IN A PICKLE

KRISTI LUNDRIGAN MYSTERY
BOOK TWO

DEBBIE MUMFORD

WDM
Publishing

COPYRIGHT

Praise for *Delectable Mountain Quilting*:
LW from Amazon: Five stars: *"Will read more of the series. Love quilting and related stuff. Story was gripping and well constructed."*

Jean from Amazon: Five stars: *"I enjoyed the easy read. A nice story with likable people. I used to quilt, so I understand the value of the antique quilt."*

Praise for *In a Pickle*:
Quilter from Amazon: Five stars: *"I'm a quilter and throughly enjoyed this story. I like a good series like this second book."*

Norrine B from Amazon: Five stars: *"Kept you on the edge of your seat. Good book for a snowy day in front of a fireplace with a warm beverage."*

Praise for *Second Sight*:
Bookgirl from Amazon: Five stars: "A lost love, a new love, psychic magic, a murder and a tiger! Wow. I loved this book. It was fast paced and easy to read. I got caught up in the "I'll just read one more chapter" syndrome and lost a bit of sleep but it

was worth it. I hope Ms. Mumford writes more in this world. I love these characters."

Dragon Slayer from Amazon: Five stars: "I liked the characters and the story line. For those that love a mystery and a good romance along with the paranormal, this book is for you."

Praise for *Sorcha's Heart*

Katie from Goodreads: Five stars: 'This story was fantastic...I strongly recommend anyone who likes paranormal dragon stories read this. Best prequel ever. Off to look for more by this author."

Old Ozark Gal from Amazon: Five stars: "...for those who enjoy a sizzling relationship without the graphic descriptions of what body part goes where, this is an excellent book. So what are you waiting for? Go read it!"

Karyn-Anne from Amazon: Five stars: "The romantic scenes were full of passion and heat, but not graphic or explicit. I really, really enjoyed this novella ... Very highly recommended!"

Ahmari from Amazon: Five stars: "This book is very well written ... I liked it so much I purchased the sequel! ... a unique idea for a

fantasy and told in a delightful manner. I look forward to reading more from this author."

Praise for *Her Highland Laird*:

Katharina from Amazon: Five stars: "I'm normally not someone who reads romance novels, but ... I stumbled over Debbie Mumford's Romance stories. This one was an absolute treat. Not only did it depict the life in 15th century correctly (well researched for such a short story), it evokes emotion very well ... I'll definitely read more by this author."

Tony from Amazon: Five stars: "Very interesting story. With some suspense and an interesting thread of love."

WEDNESDAY

Kristi Lundrigan sailed into *Delectable Mountain Quilting*, her ankle length patchwork skirt swirling around her legs. She grinned at Mattie Stebbings, one of her two sales clerks and the former owner of the quilt shop. Mattie nodded in acknowledgment as her hands were busy measuring a length of a gorgeous cerulean blue batik print for the customer who stood across the cutting table from her. The customer's hand rested possessively on a stack of six additional bolts of fabric.

Business was good. Barely past their 9:30 a.m. opening and Mattie was already preparing to cut a good-sized sale.

Kristi said, "Good morning, Mattie," before turning her attention to the customer. "Nice to see you, Elaine. Did you find everything you need?"

Elaine Hastings' freckled face and hazel eyes fairly glowed with happiness as she fingered the remaining bolts in her stack. "Oh, Kristi! I absolutely adore these new batiks you ordered. I can practically see the color wash quilt I'm going to make with them."

Mattie shook her head. "Traitor. You'd think I'd never ordered nice fabrics when I owned the store."

Kristi glanced at her clerk quickly, but was relieved to see that Mattie was smiling, her eyes on the yardage she was cutting.

Elaine shook her head, making her strawberry blonde curls dance, and laughed. "You may be my best— and oldest— friend, Mattie, but Kristi has a flair for this business, and you know it!"

Mattie slid the newly cut yardage over to Elaine to fold while she pulled the next bolt from the stack and unrolled enough to measure out her next cut. She paused for a moment, glanced at Kristi and winked. "I do know it. Best thing I ever did was sell this shop to Kristi." Her eyes clouded for a moment, and Kristi imagined Mattie was remembering the circumstances that had surrounded the sale last year: her husband's gambling debts, his subsequent death, and her mother's murder trial, conviction, and imprisonment. The petite, dark-haired woman had endured a hard year, but Mattie's life seemed to be settling into a nice rhythm now.

She shrugged and turned her attention back to the sea-foam green batik on the cutting table. "But if I can't needle my best friend, what's the point?"

All three women laughed, and Kristi continued to the combination kitchen / employee break room at the back of the store. After the initial renovations were complete and the store had been open for business for a few months, she'd asked her contractor, Mark Robards, to install a set of lockers for her employees' use. She opened one of the six square metal units now and shoved her embroidered denim shoulder bag inside, locked the door, and put the key in her pocket. She knew no one in the shop, employee or customer, would steal from her, but there was an exterior door that opened into the kitchen, and while they kept it locked…. Well, mistakes could happen. Plus, Kristi had once found a dead body on the other side of that very door.

Moving to the desk Mark had built into the space between the doors to the sales floor and the storage room, Kristi pulled her laptop computer out of its drawer and opened the inventory file.

Time to decide what fabrics to order next. The batiks had been selling well and she hoped to restock her current patterns as well as see what was new. Plus now that it was mid-July, it was time to review this year's Christmas prints, flannels and winter prints to see if there was anything she'd overlooked last month. Quilters were already planning, and buying, Christmas fabrics. After all, Christmas quilts couldn't be completed overnight!

Once she'd placed an order for two dozen bolts of fabric, Kristi closed her inventory file and opened the folder labeled *Garnet County Fair* and clicked on the scheduling spreadsheet. The fair was scheduled to start on Friday, and she still had a lot to do. She'd had to hire two temporary clerks to make sure she could cover all the shifts for both the booth at the fairgrounds and the shop's regular hours during the fair's ten day run. It had been a scheduling nightmare to ensure that the temps were always on duty with an experienced employee (herself included) no matter which venue they were assigned to cover. Thank heavens the shop was always closed on Sundays. She appreciated having two days out of the ten when she only needed to staff the booth at the fair.

Kristi had interviewed both Andrea Jansson and Eula Gibbs for the sales clerk position she'd eventually hired Ruby Andrews to fill. Kristi felt very lucky that both women had been available and willing to help out during the fair. Andrea attended community college in Billings, but was home for the summer. And Eula, a local grandmother, augmented her retirement income by selling baby quilts and knitted throws at church bazaars and craft fairs. Kristi had placed a few of Eula's baby quilts in the shop on consignment, so the two had already established a working relationship.

Satisfied with the schedule, Kristi closed the spreadsheet and opened a diagram of the booth that had been assigned to *Delectable Mountain Quilting*. She'd attended the fair in years past, but this was her first year as an exhibitor. The shop had been up and running for a few months before the fair started last year, but Kristi had felt it was too soon to attempt a booth. She'd still been ironing out the unexpected surprises that appeared in any new business. But this year... this year she had more than twelve months of retail experience under her belt and felt ready for the challenge.

"Excuse me, Kristi," a familiar voice said.

Kristi glanced up to find Elaine Hastings smiling at her from the sales floor side of the break room door. Kristi had first met Elaine at Gary Stebbings' funeral last year. Elaine had been playing the self-assigned role of Mattie's guardian, protecting the new widow from overly effusive mourners and making sure she had food and water as needed. Kristi and Elaine had hit it off immediately; Kristi appreciating Elaine's loyalty and quiet support of her friend, and Elaine liking Kristi's concern for Mattie's well-being. Since that time, they'd developed an easy friendship.

Closing her laptop and standing quickly, Kristi held out her hand to her friend. "What can I do for you, Elaine?"

Elaine accepted her proffered hand and squeezed it gently before letting it drop. "I'm sorry. I didn't mean to disturb you," she said, then grimaced and amended, "well, obviously I did, since I could see you were working and spoke anyway!"

Kristi laughed. "No worries. What's up?"

Elaine's hazel eyes twinkled and she lowered her voice to a conspiratorial whisper. "I just wanted to wish you luck at the fair." She paused, and then continued in a rush, "And to ask you for the same."

A small frown furrowed Kristi's brow. "Luck? With what?"

"Pickles!" Elaine giggled. "I finally decided to enter a jar of my *dill delights* in the fair."

"Oh! You mean those dills you served at the barbecue last month?"

Elaine nodded, her grin widening.

"Well, I'd say you're a shoo-in. Those little dills are delicious!"

"Thanks. I sure hope the judges agree."

"Let me know when the pickles come up for judging and I'll see if I can't take a break," Kristi said. Lowering her voice to her own conspiratorial whisper, she added, "After all, friends stick together!"

Elaine hugged her and whispered, "They sure do. I'll let you know the time as soon as it's announced." Elaine glanced around the shop. "I know the shop will have a booth at the fair, but are you entering anything?"

Kristi grinned. "As a matter of fact, I am... and you'll love this... you're entering pickles, and I'm entering my grandmother's Pickle Dish quilt! How's that for coincidence?"

Elaine's eyes widened and she burst out laughing. "That's too funny! I can hardly wait to see it." She paused for a moment, a small frown creasing her forehead. "Mattie is entering her Delectable Mountain quilt." She glanced over her shoulder and lowered her voice conspiratorially before continuing, "The one she made. Not the antique one that caused so much trouble last year."

Kristi nodded encouragingly, not sure what Elaine was getting at.

"Well, your quilt won't be in the same division as hers will it?"

"Nope. Nanna Van Oss's quilt was made in the '30s. It'll be in one of the antique divisions. Mattie's is contemporary."

Elaine's face cleared. "Good. Now I can cheer for both of you!"

They chatted for a few more moments before Elaine turned to leave, carrying her bag of newly purchased quilting cottons. Alone once more, Kristi opened her laptop again and made a note on the scheduling spreadsheet. Once she knew when the pickles were to be judged she'd have to make sure that both she and Mattie were available to support Elaine. After all, Mattie and

Elaine were friends of long-standing. Kristi was a new addition to their lives.

Glancing out to the sales floor, Kristi smiled, quiet pride blooming in her chest. Jewel-toned fabrics sparkled from every shelf. Beautifully made quilts hung above the shelving units, samples meant to entice quilters into upcoming classes. Pre-cut fat quarters nestled in baskets or were tied with narrow satin ribbons into colorful stacks. Everything about the store was neat and clean and inviting. Exactly the kind of quilt shop she'd hoped to create when she'd purchased *Delectable Mountain Quilting*.

Fair week would be busy, even stressful at times, but Kristi knew that she and her employees were up to the challenge. The shop's booth at Garnet County Fair was going to be a huge success!

2

THURSDAY MORNING

Kristi woke the next morning to prodding from her moggy cats. Stitches, her gray tabby female, rubbed her head against Kristi's fingers while Between, the little tuxedo male who'd been named because his claws reminded Kristi of the tiny, sharp needles used in hand quilting, batted softly at a lock of hair that had fallen across Kristi's cheek. Fortunately, his claws remained sheathed.

Gently pushing Between away from her face, she yawned and stroked both cats. Good thing she had two hands... and only two cats.

"All right, kitty-kids," she said, stifling another yawn. "I'm up. You can relax now." Shooing the purring felines away, she sat up, tucked her shoulder-length blonde hair behind her ears, and stretched. Since her alarm hadn't gone off yet, she glanced at the clock and rolled her eyes; 6:00 a.m.!

"Honestly, you two," she chided the cats who were now stretched out on the far side of the bed, "I was hoping for another hour of sleep." After cancelling her alarm, she stood and trudged to the bathroom. Best to get the day started; this was going to be a busy one.

When Kristi emerged from the bedroom— showered, neatly

dressed in her favorite burgundy slacks, a white cotton shell, and a lightweight navy cardigan, and ready for the day— Stitches and Between met her with plaintive meows.

"Seriously, kids? Breakfast is *not* late. You two are just early."

Moving carefully past the cats who were trying to wind their way between her legs, she headed to the kitchen. The moment they discerned her direction, the moggies raced ahead of her, then slowed to lead the way to their food bowls, tails high and proud.

Kristi smiled at their antics. Picking up their bowls and depositing them on the counter, she pulled a bag of kibble from the cabinet, then moved to the refrigerator. Today was their day for a small serving of canned tuna. When she placed the bowls back on the floor, Between pounced on his food. Stitches, however, chose to groom her ears and face before condescending to eat what Kristi had offered.

Kristi suppressed a giggle. Trust Stitches to remind Kristi that cats ruled!

After fixing a bowl of her favorite overnight oats and a mug of mint tea, Kristi moved to her scrubbed oak breakfast table. Glancing out the picture window above the padded window seat beside the table, she breathed a happy sigh.

The view, amazing as always, thrilled her. The mid-July day was shaping up to be a beauty. The clear blue sky seemed to stretch forever, living up to Montana's *Big Sky Country* nickname. The valley grassland was dotted with cattle, the fence lines barely discernible at this distance. The foothills stepped into the Absaroka Range's tall, craggy mountains, their slopes graduating from the dark green of pine forests to the steely blue-gray of granite peaks and precipices.

A perfect summer day in Paradise Valley… and she was going to be too busy to enjoy it!

Today was the last day before the Garnet County Fair was scheduled to begin, and it was going to be a busy one. Not only did she have a full day at *Delectable Mountain Quilting* planned, but she and her staff and friends would need to set up their booth in the exhibitors' pavilion in the late afternoon.

Turning her attention to breakfast, she savored the oat and yogurt mixture and sipped her mint tea. A day like this one required high quality fuel. As she was scraping the last oats onto her spoon, Stitches and Between leapt lightly onto the padded window seat and stared pointedly at her bowl.

"Your timing is excellent," she said, slipping the now empty bowl between them. The cats licked the remnants of yogurt greedily while Kristi finished her mint tea. "It's a good thing you two aren't spoiled or anything."

Gathering up her dishes, she carried them to the sink, washed them and put them in the rack to dry. It was still early, but she had a lot to do today. Might as well head to the shop. Decision made, she gave the kitty-kids a quick pat good-bye and, grabbing her embroidered denim shoulder bag and keys from their hooks by the back door, she sailed out the door, locked it, and marched to her bright red Subaru Outback.

"Time to get this show on the road," she murmured as she fastened her seat belt and started the engine. "Ready or not, here we come, Garnet County Fair-goers!

The day turned out much as Kristi expected. Customers and staff alike buzzed with anticipation about the fair. Quilts were discussed, of course. Who entered what in which division. Antique quilts. Contemporary quilts. Quilts designed for beds. Wall quilts, table runners, even quilted clothing. If you could imagine a quilted item, it seemed you'd find it at the fair.

In addition to quilts, quite a bit of conversation centered on the edible entries. Customers chatted about pies, cakes, canned fruits and vegetables, and the ever popular pickles and relishes. Which led right back to quilting!

"Don't forget," Kristi said loudly, to the shop as a whole, "we're going to be giving demonstrations at our fair booth, including one on how to construct Pickle Dish blocks. Mattie has flyers with dates and times of all our demos at the register, so be sure to pick one up before you leave."

"What a great tie-in to the pickle contest, Kristi," Molly Raskin said, arms loaded with bolts of pretty calicoes. "I'm hoping to take home the blue ribbon this year. Mavis Johnson has been the reigning pickle queen long enough!"

"Good luck, Molly," Kristi said with a smile. "I'm not taking sides since several of the entrants are customers."

Molly laughed. "Gotta spread the love around, right?"

"You bet. Just like with the quilts… I can hardly wait to see the exhibits, but I'm sure glad I don't have to judge!"

Molly nodded. "And you seem to be sticking with a theme this year. Didn't I hear that you entered your grandmother's Pickle Dish quilt in the antique division?"

"That's right. Her quilt served as my inspiration for our demonstrations. Plus, pickles and fairs just go together, right?"

"I definitely think so," Molly agreed. "I can hardly wait for the judging. The batch of pickles I put up this year are the best I've ever made… and my pickles are favorites with our hands out at the ranch."

"I'll be there to watch the judging, if I can work out the schedule," Kristi said, though she failed to mention that she'd be rooting for Elaine's *dill delights*. What Molly didn't know, couldn't hurt her feelings.

While they were talking, Jen Stevens joined them. "Have you heard who the judges will be?"

"I made it my mission to find out," Molly said, leaning in and lowering her voice. "My sources said there'll be three: Louisa Rizzoli, Silvi Kuhlman, and," she glanced around to make sure she wasn't overheard, "Herman Studebakker."

Kristi nodded. "Good choices. Mama Rizzoli certainly knows quality food when she tastes it." *Rizzoli's Fine Italian Restaurant* was a favorite of Kristi's.

"Yes," agreed Jen, "and *Silvi's Pie in the Sky* has baked goods to die for, though I'm not sure what that has to do with pickles."

"Quality is quality," Kristi said with a shrug. "I'm sure Silvi will do a great job."

"The one I'm not sure about is Herman Studebakker," Molly said, her tone a little disapproving. "How does owning *The Honey Barrel Brewpub* qualify him to judge pickles?"

Jen laughed. "You obviously haven't been around the guys who hail from the Midwest. They swear by pickles and beer. Claim that adding a splash of pickle juice to their beer makes it that much better."

Kristi nodded. "I've even known people who skewer pickle slices and add them to beer as a garnish."

Molly's eyes widened. "Okay... so maybe Herman is a natural."

They shared another laugh, then Molly and Jen moved to the cutting table while Kristi took her turn at the cash register.

Pickles and quilts. This was going to be a fair to remember!

3

THURSDAY AFTERNOON

When 4:00 p.m. finally arrived, Kristi turned the sign on the front window from "Open" to "Closed" and locked the door. Turning to Mattie and Ruby, her sales staff, she grinned and said, "Okay. Now the real work begins!"

The women pulled flattened boxes and folding display tables from the storeroom. The tables were stacked in the kitchen near the back door, while the boxes were carried to the display floor. Once boxes had been reassembled, the packing began. Bolts of fabric, selected in advance, were wrapped in plastic and stacked in large boxes. Rotary cutting tools, books, and notions filled several more. Everything they'd need to set up *Delectable Mountain Quilting's* booth at the fair was considered and stowed in boxes.

Kristi packed quilts for display, including a few that would be available for sale. She smiled as she folded the sample Pickle Dish quilt that would promote an upcoming class. She hoped to attract several new students from among the fair-goers who visited the booth.

Mattie packed the Viking sewing machine and portable table

Kristi would use to demonstrate the construction of a Pickle Dish block, while Ruby gathered everything she and Mattie would need for their hand quilting demonstrations. Since they wouldn't have space for a full-size quilting frame, she chose several hoops of varying sizes.

Just as they finished moving the boxes to the kitchen, the back door opened to admit Jason Reynolds, Stacy Akins Robards, and her new husband, Mark Robards.

"Reinforcements have arrived," Mattie called over her shoulder to the display floor where Kristi and Ruby were making sure the shop was still presentable for tomorrow's customers.

Kristi raced to the kitchen, hugged Jason— the man might be her ex-husband, but they'd been dating again for over a year now — and shook hands with Mark and Stacy, her former contractor and his new wife, who just happened to be Kristi's best friend. Kristi and Jason had witnessed Mark and Stacy's engagement last Christmas, and had stood up for them at their wedding just a few weeks ago.

"Welcome," she said, smiling, "and thanks again for volunteering to help us get set up at the fairgrounds."

"No problem," Mark said. "Are these the boxes you need loaded?"

"They are indeed," Mattie said. "Choose a vehicle and stack them in."

Jason nodded, rubbed his hands together, and took charge. "The weather looks good, and we're not going far, so I think we're safe to transport the closed boxes, tables, and other large items in the bed of Mark's truck. Let's put the bolts of fabric in Kristi's Subaru and Stacy's Taurus. Everything else can go wherever you can find room."

"My thoughts exactly," Kristi agreed. "Okay, let's get this stuff loaded." Ruby blocked the back door open while Jason and Mark hefted the folding tables.

With six willing workers, the loading went quickly and

smoothly. Soon the cars were caravanning their way across town to the fairgrounds. When they arrived, they parked in the exhibitor's loading zone. Kristi signed in with the administrators in charge of set-up and then led the way to their assigned booth.

The fair committee had done a great job of delineating the booths. Panels hung with dark background curtains divided the booths from one another. Kristi had paid for a double booth on a corner, so they had a good amount of space to work with.

"All right," she said, "let's bring the tables in first." Pulling a diagram out of her shoulder bag, she handed it to Mark. "This is the way I'd like them arranged. That smaller rectangle shows the placement of my sewing machine and its table."

Mark nodded and passed the diagram to Jason. "Looks good. Shall we grab some tables?" Everyone but Kristi and Mattie followed him out to the truck.

"What do you think about the display quilts?" Kristi asked Mattie.

Mattie looked the area over carefully before answering. "Let's save those for last. We'll have a better idea what should go where when the fabric and notions have been arranged." She paused, considered the traffic flow, and said, "But offhand I think the Pickle Dish should go on that background... near where you'll be demoing the blocks."

Kristi nodded. "That's a good idea. Plus it'll stand out to folks just wandering the aisles. Might draw some into the booth."

The group worked well together. Once the tables were placed and covered with floor length cloths, Jason and Mark took over hauling boxes inside, while Kristi, Mattie, and Ruby arranged the merchandise and Stacy broke the emptied boxes down and stored them under the tables.

By 7:00 p.m. the booth was complete. Gorgeous quilting cottons stood in perfect rows with baskets of pre-cut fat quarters scattered around the various displays. A small bookshelf held books on design and quilt patterns, and beautifully crafted quilts hung on every backdrop. A single table stood empty at one side of the open corner of the booth: their cutting table. Kristi hoped that one would be busy for the duration of the fair. They'd be making do with electronic tablets and a locking cash box in lieu of a cash register, but Kristi felt confident her staff was up to the challenge.

When all was in readiness, Kristi handed Mattie and Ruby their exhibitor badges and they said their good-byes.

"Remember…"Kristi began, but before she could finish her thought, Ruby interrupted her.

"We know. We know. Mattie will open *Delectable Mountain Quilting* in the morning."

"And," Mattie added, "I'll call Andrea tonight to make sure she remembers she's scheduled to help me in the shop tomorrow." She grinned at Kristi. "Don't worry. We'll hold down the fort!"

Kristi smiled, delighted that the college girl had been willing to help out for the duration of the fair.

Before Kristi could make a sound, Ruby continued, "And I'll be here bright and early in the morning to take my first shift here at the fair." She laughed. "I won't have bells on, but I will be wearing this!" She waved her exhibitor's badge at Kristi.

"Perfect," Kristi said. "I'll be here too. Hopefully both sites will have profitable days."

All six of them walked from the exhibitor's hall to the parking lot, and Kristi and Jason, Mark and Stacy waved as Mattie and Ruby drove away.

"Well," Jason said, "a good evening's work." He placed an arm around Kristi's shoulders. "Your booth looks great and you're ready for the fair."

"Yes," she nodded. "I think we are. I'm still a bit nervous, but I think we'll be fine."

Stacy nodded. "I'm sure of it. Your first fair experience is going to be a great one."

"I agree," Mark chimed in, "but that's for tomorrow. Right now, how about we grab some dinner? Anyone up for Italian?"

"Always," Jason agreed, rubbing his belly. "Nothing like loading and unloading to work up an appetite."

"Great," Mark said. "Let's head to *Rizzoli's* and finish this conversation over pasta and wine."

4

THURSDAY EVENING

Jason and Kristi stepped into *Rizzoli's Fine Italian Restaurant*. After checking to make sure Stacy and Mark didn't already have a table reserved, they settled into one of the comfortable, high-backed booths. Kristi leaned back against the padded seat, closed her eyes, and sighed contentedly. It had been a busy, non-stop day and she was more than ready to relax.

Rizzoli's, with its red-checked tablecloths, raffia covered wine bottle candle holders, soft recorded music, and mellow atmosphere, was just what she needed. Plus, Kristi loved their pasta dishes. Homemade pasta topped with rich tomato sauce, perfectly spiced meat, and gooey cheese spelled comfort food to die for!

Jason put his arm around her and drew her close— a definite benefit of booth over table. "Don't get too comfortable," he whispered. "You don't want to fall asleep before Mark and Stacy even get here."

She nestled her head against his shoulder and smiled. "What? And miss dinner? Not a chance!"

He kissed the top of her head, then gently withdrew his arm. "They're here."

Kristi straightened and greeted their friends. "Welcome, you two. Thanks again for all your hard work today!"

Jason rose and shook hands with Mark while Stacy slid into the booth opposite Kristi.

"No problem," Mark said. "Glad to help."

"Sorry to keep you waiting," Stacy added. "We stopped home long enough to drop off Mark's truck. No need to have two vehicles here at the restaurant."

Kristi shook her head. "We've only been here a minute or two."

"Yep. Kristi hadn't even had time to fall asleep yet," Jason said with a grin and slid sideways just enough to avoid the swat Kristi sent in his direction.

All four were laughing as Mama Rizzoli herself appeared at their table. The plump, gray haired woman beamed at them. "Good! You're having fun already," she said, handing each of them a menu. "Tonight's special is chicken marsala with fettuccine," she kissed her fingertips before spreading them wide in a *chef's kiss*, "but everything on the menu is good. I'll get you a carafe of water while you make your choices."

A remarkably few minutes after taking their orders, Mama Rizzoli reappeared with their meals. She strode among the tables like a queen, while a dark-haired teenage boy followed in her wake bearing a large tray with their plates balanced on one hand and a folding serving stand in the other. As he opened the stand with a snap and deposited his tray on it, another young man approached with two bottles of wine and four stemmed wine glasses.

Mama Rizzoli nodded and both young men returned to the kitchen.

"Now," Mama said with a clap, "your dinners!"

She placed a steaming plate of shrimp Alfredo in front of Kristi, who inhaled in delight. Glorious fettuccine noodles smothered in creamy, cheesy, white sauce and covered with perfectly sautéed shrimp. Kristi's mouth watered just looking at it, but she forced herself to wait until the others were served.

Stacy had chosen cheese ravioli, and her plate looked just as appetizing as Kristi's.

Jason and Mark had both decided on meat dishes with tomato sauce. Jason, as he nearly always did, chose spaghetti and meatballs. As he liked to say when Kristie teased him about his lack of variety, "why mess with perfection?"

Mark decided on Mama's classic lasagna, and Kristi knew from experience it was an excellent choice. Perfectly spiced beef, rich tomato sauce, and cheese so gooey a person could make a meal of it on its own.

Generous tossed salads and slices of freshly baked focaccia bread completed the meal. Since the four friends were having both white and red sauces, Jason ordered two wines: their favorite chianti and a nice pinot gris.

For the next quarter hour, the only sounds emanating from their table were the clink of silverware and stemware and the contented sighs of hunger being satisfied.

When her shrimp Alfredo had been decimated, Kristi leaned back against the padded bench seat and watched as Jason chased the last bite of spaghetti sauce with a piece of focaccia. Stacy was also leaning back, sipping from her glass of pinot gris, while Mark stabbed the final bit of his lasagna and popped it into his mouth.

"Now *that* was a meal," Jason said, leaning back and patting his stomach.

Almost as if she'd been watching the group's progress, Mama Rizzoli appeared beside the booth. "Good?" she asked. One look at their satisfied smiles and she pronounced, "Good! Now, who wants dessert?"

Everyone demurred at once.

"I couldn't eat another bite," Stacy said.

"Me neither," Kristi agreed, "but we would take coffee all around."

"Coffee sounds great, but no dessert for me," Jason said, then he glanced at Mark and narrowed his eyes. "Unless you're considering a challenge?"

"Who? Me?" Mark asked, eyes sparkling with mischief. Stacy elbowed him in the ribs and he laughed. "Guess I'll pass... this time."

Jason laughed, and Mama Rizzoli shook her head.

"Boys!" she said, looking from Kristi to Stacy. "They never grow up."

"Hey, now," Jason objected. "You're talking about the sheriff, you know."

Mama turned away with a sniff. "I know," she said over her shoulder, "and I repeat, *boys!*"

Stacy and Kristi giggled, while Mark and Jason scowled at Mama's retreating back. Then the two men glanced at each other and laughed.

"She knows us too well," Mark said after a moment.

"Agreed," said Jason.

When Mama Rizzoli returned with a carafe of coffee and four mugs, Kristi smiled and asked, "You're judging food exhibits at the fair, aren't you? Are you excited?"

Mama beamed as she poured their coffee. "I am! It's an honor to be invited to judge, and I'm looking forward to it."

"What will you be judging?" Stacy asked.

"I'm slated for two divisions in canning: pickles and jams; and two in baking: pies and cakes."

"Where do I sign up?" Mark quipped. "I *love* cakes and pies!"

Jason puffed out his chest and tapped his badge. "I think the sheriff should be asked. Sounds like hazardous duty."

Mama laughed. "I'll be sure to tell the committee you two are interested for next year's event."

Kristi rolled her eyes, but ignored the men and continued her chat with Mama. "Do you know who you'll be judging with?"

Mama distributed the mugs of coffee with a nod. "The committee decided on three judges for each division." She glanced at Jason. "Three avoids a tie." Turning her attention back to Kristi, she continued, "For the canning division, I'll be working with Herman Studebakker and Silvi Kuhlman. For baking, Silvi and I will be joined by Emma Marsten."

Stacy nodded. "Good choices, especially for baking. Nobody knows pies and cakes like Silvi, and isn't Emma a past grand prize winner?"

Mama laughed. "She is. The committee had to disqualify Emma from entering— she's won too many times!— so they asked her to judge instead."

"Smart," said Mark. "Let's other people have a chance while not alienating the past winner."

Mama cocked her head and eyed Kristi. "Why the interest? You're not entering one of my divisions, are you?"

"Heavens no," Kristi said as Jason nearly choked on his coffee. She glared at him, but patted his back. "I'm no cook, but I do have some friends who are entering."

"Kristi will be busy with her booth anyway," Stacy added.

"Really? Your shop will have a booth this year?"

Kristi nodded. "Our very first. I hope you'll stop by when you have a minute."

Mama smiled. "Of course! We have to support our local businesses." Placing the carafe of coffee in the center of the table, she turned to leave. "Have fun at the fair."

5

FRIDAY MORNING

The first day of the Garnet County Fair dawned clear and gorgeous, and Kristi was up to greet the sunrise. Stitches and Between, her moggy cats, didn't even have a chance to purr her awake. She was simply too excited to sleep in.

"This is it, kitty-kids," she practically sang as she dressed in her favorite ankle-length patchwork skirt and pale gold cotton shell top. "The fair starts today!"

She leaned down to stroke Stitches, who had stretched out on the bed while Kristi dressed, before following Between from the room. The little tuxedo male strutted toward the kitchen, tail held high. Clearly, he'd decided it was time for breakfast.

"Sorry, Between," Kristi called as she stepped into her quilting studio. "You'll have to wait another minute or two."

Rummaging through the top drawer of her sewing cabinet, she pulled out her quilter's chatelaine and hung it around her neck. Made of a lovely batik cotton and padded with batting, the chatelaine always reminded her of a priest's stole, though not nearly as long. With ribbons and pockets for all her favorite quilting tools, the chatelaine insured she was never without her small scissors, seam ripper, or neutral colored thread. It even had a small pincushion.

She rarely used it at home where all of her tools were already handy, but for classes or sewing circles, her chatelaine was indispensable. And today, at the fair, it would not only keep her organized, but would serve as a conversation starter. Especially when she left her booth to wander through the fair's other attractions.

Between meowed plaintively from the studio doorway. Kristi rolled her eyes as she finished tying her scissors on their assigned ribbon.

"Alright, kids," she said, patting the chatelaine into place around her neck. "I'm ready to get your breakfast now."

Striding to the kitchen with both cats racing ahead, Kristi considered her own breakfast. She wasn't really hungry— she was too anxious to get to the fairgrounds and make sure her booth was ready for the day— but knew she should eat a healthy breakfast. After all, the rest of the day was likely to be filled with fair food, and while she loved funnel cakes and deep-fried Oreos as much as the next person, they weren't exactly nutritious.

While she mulled over her own choices, she poured kibble into dishes for the kitty-kids and placed them in their assigned spots. The cats pounced on their food as if they hadn't eaten in weeks.

"Oh, come on, you two! You can't have been that hungry. Not when you had a saucer of milk with your dinner last night."

Neither cat so much as glanced at her.

"Fine. Be that way. Now, what to fix for myself…"

She finally settled on granola mixed with peach yogurt, a sliced banana, and a tall glass of orange juice. She tried to take her time, savor the flavors and textures while she admired the view of the Absaroka Mountain range from the wide window beside her breakfast table, but she was too distracted to do more than shovel the food into her mouth.

When her dishes were washed and stacked in the rack to dry, Kristi grabbed her embroidered denim shoulder bag, yanked her keys from the rack by the back door and called a hurried good-bye to the cats.

At last! She was on her way to the fair!

6

FRIDAY NOON

What a great start to the fair!

The *Delectable Mountain Quilting* booth was a definite success. Loyal customers stopped by to see what Kristi and her staff had brought to the fair and fair-goers who had never set foot in her shop stopped to browse and ask questions about quilting. A few even took flyers and said they'd be back to watch the demonstrations.

Kristi was thrilled. Potential new customers was one of the reasons she'd decided to go to the trouble and expense of having a booth. And this was just the first day!

When she finished her first demo— how to machine piece a Pickle Dish block, Kristi took a breather. The initial flood of visitors had ebbed, so she checked in with Ruby.

"Will you be okay if I take a walk and check out the other vendors?" she asked Ruby.

"Absolutely. You deserve a break after that demo," Ruby said. "Plus, I want to be able to look around after while too." She grinned. "You go first, then you can tell me where the good stuff is."

Kristi laughed, then stood, stretched her back, and pulled her denim shoulder bag from beneath the table skirt where they'd stowed their personal items.

"I won't be too long. I want you to take your break before Stacy gets here. She and I are going to go to lunch over at the food court."

Ruby nodded. "Fair food is the best, though it's a good thing it only comes around once a year."

With a final wave, Kristi stepped out of the booth and into the crowd milling around in the wide main corridor. The vendors who had booths at the fair were a varied bunch. There were a few local businesses, like Kristi's, but most were national brands that followed the fair circuit hoping to make sales in areas where their products weren't available on a daily basis.

She was particularly interested in the booths that featured sewing machines and custom furniture like sewing cabinets, cutting tables, and big ironing boards. And then there were the professional quilting machines! Kristi practically drooled over those. She dreamed of owning one. They were too big for her quilting studio at home, but someday she hoped to house one in the shop.

She couldn't justify the expense yet, *Delectable Mountain Quilting* was still in its infancy, but eventually....

Forcing herself away from the sewing-related vendors, Kristi browsed through book booths, jewelry displays, booths devoted to wood and pellet stoves, and the ever-present real estate and insurance displays. She'd covered about half of the exhibits when she glanced at her watch and decided she'd best get back to work. After all, Ruby deserved a break too.

"Your turn," she told Ruby as she stuffed her shoulder bag back beneath the table. "Be sure to check out the quilting machines. I want to buy one eventually and I'd like your take on which brand and model I should choose."

"You bet! I'd love to learn to use one of those monsters," Ruby quipped. Then, with a wave, she disappeared into the crowd.

Alone in the booth, Kristi chatted with browsers, made a few sales— cutting and folding the fabric and ringing up the charges without assistance— and advised a couple of newbies on the best classes for someone with no prior quilting (or sewing, for that matter!) experience.

She enjoyed herself immensely. Kristi was nothing if not a people person. When a lull occurred, she plopped into the folding chair beside her sewing table and drank from the water bottle she'd stashed in the sewing basket that held supplies for her demos.

"You look a little flushed," a voice said from behind her. "Busy morning?"

Kristi turned to find that Stacy had entered the booth from the far corner. Grinning, she returned the water bottle to her sewing basket.

"It's been busy," Kristi agreed, "but that's great since the whole point of the booth is to meet people and make connections."

"And sales," Stacy nodded. "Don't forget the sales."

"Definitely," Kristi agreed with a laugh, "and we've had a good number of those, too, this morning. And it's only the first day!"

Just then Ruby appeared. "Hey, Stacy. Welcome to our home away from home." Before Stacy could reply, Ruby turned to Kristi. "I'm back, all rested and refreshed and rarin' to go. You and Stacy go have lunch. If you bring me back a corndog, I won't need to take another break until later this afternoon."

"Deal," agreed Kristi. "If you get swamped, text me and I'll head straight back."

"Will do," Ruby said with a nod, "but I doubt there'll be anything I can't handle."

Grabbing her shoulder bag from its hiding spot, Kristi joined Stacy in the aisle, where they blended into the throng of shoppers and browsers.

"Food court okay with you?" Stacy asked.

"You bet. I look forward to funnel cakes and deep-fried Oreos all year!"

Stacy laughed. "I hope you're planning to eat something other than sweets for lunch."

"Yes, *Mom*," she replied, sticking her tongue out at her friend.

They walked as quickly as they could, darting among the many people who stopped without warning to point and chat. Kristi imagined herself as a minnow, racing upstream while avoiding rocks and bigger fish.

When they reached the door to the exhibitor's building, they stepped outside into a beautiful summer day. Blue sky, puffy white clouds, and warm sunshine. Birdsong would've made the picture complete, but the little creatures couldn't compete with the sounds of the fair. Cattle and other critters in the livestock barns competed with the mechanical noises, not to mention screams of delight from the rides on the midway. It might only be noon, but the carnival portion of the fair was in full swing.

Then there were the odors. The earthy scents of farm animals mingled with car exhaust and cotton candy sweetness. All in all, stepping outside the confines of the exhibitor's building resulted in a sensory overload.

The two friends took deep breaths, grinned at each other, and headed toward the building that housed the food court as well as the many food related competitions. Cooking, baking, canning, pickling... all the food related arts were represented at this year's fair. There was even a division for cake decorating! Kristi couldn't wait to wander through the aisles and admire all of the various entries.

But first, lunch!

The two women got in line at the window that advertised corndogs, hamburgers, and other more substantial foods. Funnel cakes and cotton candy would have to wait for later.

They were early enough that the line moved quickly. Stacy ordered a cheeseburger, onion rings, and a strawberry lemonade. Kristi eyed the loaded waffle fries— waffle-cut fries smoth-ered in cheddar cheese, green onions, and bacon bits and flavored with steak seasoning—but finally decided on a State Fair Sub.

After paying, they moved to the next window to await their orders. When the young woman behind the counter handed Kristi her sub and cola, she barely kept from drooling. The State Fair Sub was cheesy, oniony, and filled with juicy Italian sausage, and smelled absolutely delicious. And that didn't even consider the crispy French bread.

Yum!

Stacy found an open two-top table and they dug into their meals. After several satisfying bites, Kristi asked what Stacy had been up to all morning.

Taking a sip of her lemonade, Stacy considered her answer. "Mark is working on a home renovation on one of the outlying ranches, so I fixed him a lunch and practically pushed him out the door." She swiped an onion ring through a puddle of ketchup and popped it into her mouth before continuing. "Then I got ready for a day at the fair."

Kristi nodded, chewing a bite of her sub. The cheese and onions perfectly complimented the tangy sausage, and she savored the flavors. After swallowing, she sipped her ice-cold cola before asking, "Have you walked through the exhibit hall yet?"

Stacy shook her head. "So far all I've seen are the livestock barns. Have you done that yet?"

"Nope. I've got a date with Jason to see the livestock later this afternoon." After another flavorful bite of her sub, Kristi asked, "What do you want to do when we finish eating?"

After blotting her lips with her napkin, Stacy answered. "Let's stick with food and go wander through the baking and canning exhibits."

"Deal. I always feel like I should be more industrious when I see all those gleaming jars of canned food. It'll be good to have moral support while I wander."

Stacy laughed. "Me too! Although when I'd find time to can, I have no idea."

"The baking isn't so bad," Kristi agreed. "I mean, I don't create works of art like we'll see in the those exhibits, but I can bake a cake." She paused, grimaced, and continued, "Pies, not so much."

"Oh, I can manage a decent pie crust, and cakes are a snap, but I agree, I wouldn't dream of entering any of my baked goods in the fair. I'll stick to real estate, thank you very much."

The two women smiled at each other, content in the knowledge that their skills lay in very different areas, before clearing their table and heading off to examine the culinary wonders produced by others.

7

FRIDAY AFTERNOON

Later that afternoon, Kristi handled sales while Ruby demonstrated hand quilting. The young woman sat in a folding chair, surrounded by others eager to learn, or at least observe, the time-honored skill of securing the three layers of a quilt together.

Ruby explained the process as she worked. "You'll notice I've secured my quilt in a hoop. When I'm at home, I prefer a quilt frame, but we don't have space here in the booth, so a hoop is a great alternative. It's portable and easy to use."

"It looks like an embroidery hoop," one woman said. "Can I use one of those?"

Ruby shook her head. "I wouldn't recommend it. You're likely to split an embroidery hoop. Notice how thick the rim is on this quilt hoop. It's not only larger and sturdier than its embroidery counterpart, it's also made of hardwood. Much stronger."

"It has to be," another onlooker piped up, "to hold all three layers together."

"Yes," agreed Ruby. "Remember the hoop is keeping three layers aligned, the pieced top, the batting, and the backing."

"Why use a hoop at all?" asked another. "Couldn't you just hold the quilt in your lap and sew?"

"Again, I wouldn't recommend it," Ruby said, loading stitches on her between. "Keeping the quilt stretched in the hoop will allow you to get smaller, more even stitches." She pulled the needle and thread through the quilt, then paused to let the others observe the stitches she'd just created.

As the women oohed and aahed over the tiny stitches, Ruby continued her lesson. "Now, besides the hoop, and the quilt of course, the other necessary tools for hand quilting are the needle, a between, which you'll notice is short with a large eye, a thimble to protect your finger as you push the needle through all those layers, and the quilting thread."

"Quilting thread?" someone asked.

"Quilting thread," Ruby stated. "I prefer mine to be 100% cotton, but no matter which type you choose, quilting thread is stronger and longer-lasting than plain sewing thread, so be careful what you buy."

"Of course," Kristi added from the cutting table where she was measuring a length of bright yellow fabric, "if you frequent a quilt shop, like *Delectable Mountain Quilting*, and tell us what you're working on, we'll be happy to advise you."

Ruby grinned. "Absolutely! I won't let you buy regular thread if I know you're hand quilting."

Ruby continued her lesson, demonstrating how to load the needle, short as it was, with several stitches and using the thimble she wore on her middle finger to push the needle through the layers.

"And that's really all there is to it," she said as she loaded the needle once again. "You hold the needle between your thumb and index finger, then position your other hand under the quilt, with the tip of your index finger right where the needle will come through the quilt back. With the needle angled slightly away from you, push the needle through the layers until you feel the tip of the needle beneath the quilt."

"Don't push too hard," a spectator added. "You don't want to prick your finger and end up with blood on the back of the quilt."

"True," Ruby said with a laugh, "although that will probably happen as you're learning. A good reason to practice on a simple quilt you're not planning to enter in the fair."

"That," agreed Kristi with a smile, "and it'll take a while to perfect your stitches. Don't expect to make tiny even stitches like Ruby's right away. Like any other skill, it takes practice."

The onlookers continued to cluster around Ruby, watching her technique and asking questions, until the alarm on her cell phone sounded, signaling the end of the demonstration.

"I could sit here and quilt all afternoon, but it's time for me to get back to work," she said as she packed up her tools and placed the hooped quilt on a nearby table so folks could continue to study her stitches. "But that doesn't mean I can't answer questions, so if you think of anything else, feel free to ask away."

The cluster of viewers thanked Ruby and broke apart. Many left the booth, but several stayed to shop and chat.

"Nicely done," Kristi murmured when Ruby joined her at the cutting table.

"Thanks," Ruby said with a smile. "I enjoyed myself. I hope all of my demos go that well."

"I'm sure they will. You're a natural teacher."

"Say, don't you have a date with the sheriff?" Ruby asked.

Kristi blushed. "I wouldn't call it a date, exactly."

Ruby cocked her head and raised an eyebrow.

"Okay," Kristi said with a laugh. "Yes. I'm meeting Jason to visit the animal exhibits."

"Well, I'm fine here, so you should get a move on," Ruby said as she made a shooing motion.

"Fine, but I'll be back in time for you to take another break before we close up for the night."

"Great. Now go have fun with your handsome sheriff."

Still blushing, Kristi grabbed her denim shoulder bag from its hiding place beneath the table and made her escape. Outside the exhibitor's building the day was still warm and sunny, but somehow the sunshine was... softer... than it had been when she'd been outside with Stacy at noon.

Taking a deep breath of air laced with the earthy scents of farm animals and automotive exhaust, as well as the carnival scents of cotton candy and axle grease, Kristi shaded her eyes and looked around for Jason. Almost immediately she spied him strolling toward her across the open space between the exhibit buildings. Her heart skipped a beat and she smiled. He certainly cut a fine figure in blue jeans, his long-sleeved, khaki uniform shirt, and his official Stetson. She watched as he touched the brim of his hat, acknowledging two women who stopped to speak to him.

Kristi sighed. She was a lucky woman to love such a man... and to be loved by him in return. Sure, they'd had their troubles — she'd divorced him a little over two years ago due to infidelity, but they'd gotten back together again a year ago last May when he'd saved her life. They'd both realized at that moment that they still loved each other and wanted nothing more than to try again.

Their relationship had been healing and growing stronger ever since.

Now she took a moment to appreciate what a handsome man her sheriff was. Tall, well-built without being too heavily muscled, he filled out his uniform very nicely. She could almost feel the texture of his wavy chestnut hair and see the gray of his eyes. Those eyes could shift from steely when he was in cop mode to a soft, almost-blue when his emotions ran high. Kristi loved his eyes.

She laughed at herself. Truth be told, she loved everything about the man! Especially now that he'd decided he wanted to be hers alone.

He finished his conversation and made his way to Kristi.

"Hello, beautiful," he said, his baritone voice pitched low for her ears alone. He didn't kiss her as she would've liked, but then he rarely indulged in public displays of affection when he was in uniform.

"Hello, yourself," she answered. "How has your day been? Any trouble at the fair?"

He grinned. "Not even a fistfight between kids." He shook his head. "We'll likely have a few calls tonight from the midway, but I doubt anything serious will occur."

As they meandered toward the animal barns, he asked, "What about you? Has your first day at the fair gone well?"

"We've had a great first day," she said and launched into a detailed description of the booth's successes, including how well-received the demos she and Ruby had given had been. "And tomorrow, Mattie will join me here at the fair, while Ruby works at the shop. Eula will come in for a couple of hours in the morning so that Mattie and I can both go root for Elaine while her pickles are being judged."

Jason smiled. "I'm glad you're feeling good about everything." He led her into the cool shade of an open-air barn. They stopped just inside to give their eyes a chance to adjust to the lower light after the brightness of the summer afternoon.

After a moment, Jason pointed out the highlights.

"This is the 4-H barn," he said. "The animals here will change on a daily basis depending on what categories the kids are showing." He pulled a tri-fold pamphlet from his back pocket and showed her the schedule. "Today they've been showing goats, but I think all of the arena work is over by now."

Kristi nodded. "I'll have to try to make it to the show ring at some point this week. Several of my customers have kids in 4-H and they've told me how hard the kids work on perfecting their control of their animals and general showmanship."

"It's not as easy as the kids make it look," Jason said. "But it's great experience for our future farmers and ranchers." He led her into the aisle between pens filled with goats of every color. "Look, here's a blue ribbon winner."

Sure enough a bright blue rosette ribbon hung on the post beside a pen holding a brown and white goat, not much bigger than a good-sized dog. The critter had horns, but Kristi wasn't sure whether or not that indicated it was a male. Reading the information card attached to the pen, she learned that this one was a doe and belonged to a twelve-year-old girl whose last name Kristi didn't recognize. Probably not one of her customers' kids, then.

After admiring the 4-H goats, they moved on to the cattle barns. Jason impressed her with his knowledge of the various breeds. From Angus to Simmental to Dexter, Jason knew the characteristics and which ranches specialized in which breeds.

They ended their tour of beef cattle with a visit to a shaggy little red cow. The animal was considerably smaller than the other cows she'd seen, with a shock of mane falling across its eyes.

"What is it?" she asked, turning to face Jason.

"That's a Highland cow," he said. "They're becoming quite popular in the States, and especially here in Montana due to their cold weather hardiness." He cocked his head and grinned at her. "They're from Scotland originally."

"Huh," she said, "well this one is certainly a cutie."

Jason rolled his eyes. "And that's what all the ranchers are concerned with... cuteness."

She swatted his arm and laughed. "Okay, what's next?"

"Your choice," he said as they emerged into the sunshine. "Horses are in that barn," he pointed to their left, "and sheep are over there," he pointed to another open-air barn to their right. "What's your pleasure?"

"Horses, definitely."

"Then horses it shall be!"

They wandered through the horse barn where Kristi saw

Arabians, quarter horses, and saddlebred horses in every color imaginable. From buckskin to black, roan to the silvery gray with black spots of an appaloosa, they were all beautiful in her estimation.

"Which was your favorite?" Jason asked.

"Oh! They're all gorgeous, but for me, it's a toss up between that buckskin and the appaloosa." She sighed and glanced again at her two favorites. "I've always loved the buckskin's light tan color with the dark mane and tail... and the dark socks! But appaloosas," she sighed again. "Such pretty coats with all those spots, and a great Native American history."

Jason nodded. "The appaloosas have a special place in my heart too. Born and bred right here in the American West by the people who made this land what it is."

"Your turn," Kristi said. "Which horse did you like best?"

"Well," he said, turning around and studying the barn. From its packed dirt central aisle, to the stalls' half-doors— many with their occupant's head hanging over the top watching the fair-goers and hoping for a treat or pats— the barn was filled to over-flowing with the quiet camaraderie of people who loved horses. "For me, it's more about how I feel in the saddle than how the horse looks."

Kristi cocked her head and raised an eyebrow.

Jason laughed. "Okay, okay. On pure aesthetics, I'd have to say that blue roan of Ethan Richardson's is my choice. Beautiful animal."

She nodded. "I've never understood the term *blue roan* until today, but that black horse really does have a blue cast to its coat. Very pretty."

"*Very pretty.*" Jason rolled his eyes. "The breeder would not be pleased with that assessment."

"Hey! I don't claim to be an expert on horses," she said, frowning and pretending to be offended. She couldn't pull it off though. A moment later she grinned at him and continued, "But I *am* an expert on quilts."

He swept off his Stetson and bowed to her. Straightening, he said, "Point taken. Can I make up for my careless words with a cup of coffee or a deep-fried Oreo?"

She linked arms with her handsome sheriff and nudged him toward the building that housed the food court. "I think an Oreo should repair my wounded feelings."

He grinned. "Then an Oreo you shall have!"

8

SATURDAY MORNING

"All right, kitty-kids," Kristi called as she grabbed her car keys and denim shoulder bag from their respective hooks by her back door. "Think good thoughts for Elaine. Her *dill delights* are being judged later this morning."

Stitches and Between looked thoroughly unimpressed as they sprawled on the cool linoleum of the kitchen floor. They'd enjoyed their breakfast, now it was nap time. Kristi was no longer a necessary part of their morning.

Shaking her head, but smiling, Kristi closed and locked the door and hopped into her bright red Subaru Outback. A few short minutes later, she parked in the exhibitor's lot at the fairgrounds, locked her car, and dropped her badge's lanyard over her head. Arriving at the *Delectable Mountain Quilting* booth, she was pleased to see that both Mattie Stebbings and Eula Gibbs had already arrived.

Mattie, shop clerk extraordinaire, was also the former owner of *Delectable Mountain Quilting* and Kristi felt lucky to have her on staff. A petite woman, with a trim physique, short, curly, dark hair, and wide brown eyes, Mattie had suffered the violent death of her husband just as the sale of her quilt shop to Kristi was closing. To make matters even more traumatic, it turned out her own mother had killed the man!

Eula Gibbs, a local grandmother and a talented quilter, often sold her hand-stitched baby quilts in the shop on consignment. Kristi had been thrilled when Eula had agreed to help out during the fair.

As the three women set up for the morning, Kristi brought them up to date on yesterday's booth activity. "So all in all," she finished, "it was a great start to our fair week."

Mattie and Eula nodded their agreement.

"Sounds like it," Eula said. "I hope today is every bit as successful."

"I'm sure it will be," Mattie said.

Kristi studied Eula. The gray-haired senior looked the part of the quintessential grandmother. She stood barely five feet tall, was nearly as wide as she was tall, and behind her wire-rimmed glasses her soft features fairly glowed with motherly comfort and charm. She looked about as intimidating as Mrs. Santa!

"Eula, are you sure you'll be comfortable working alone while Mattie and I watch the pickle judging?"

Mattie turned from arranging fat quarters in color fans, her dark eyes wide with concern. Kristi smiled reassuringly at her. If one of them needed to stay behind to help Eula, Kristi would do it. Elaine had been Mattie's best friend since childhood. Kristi was a newcomer to their lives.

Eula, however, relieved their minds. Waving her hands to include the entire exhibitor building, she said, "I'll be fine! What could happen to me with all these good people around?"

"But what if things get busy?" Kristi asked, still not sure her temporary employee was up to being left on her own.

"Pshaw. Then people will wait a bit longer than I'd like." She waved away Kristi's concern. "Quilters are generous, caring people. They'll take it in stride."

Mattie nodded, her dark curls bobbing. "That's true, Kristi.

Our regulars would be more likely to offer to help than to get upset."

"True enough," Kristi agreed with a smile. "Okay. We'll stick with the schedule as planned." She pointed a finger at Eula. "But if you feel overwhelmed, text me. Agreed?"

Eula beamed at her, but nodded. "Agreed."

A few minutes later Kristi and Mattie arrived at the judging area for the canning division. There was a small stage in front of the dark blue curtain divider that delineated the area. Several rows of folding chairs faced the judges' table and a smaller table to the side held the jars of pickles to be judged.

A quick scan of the assembled spectators found Elaine fidgeting in her seat in the front row. Kristi and Mattie exchanged a glance, grinned, and hurried to join their friend.

"You came!" Elaine bounced from her seat and hugged Mattie before grabbing Kristi and hugging her so hard she nearly lost her balance. "Thank you! I really need someone to hold my hand to keep me from jumping up and running from the building screaming at the top of my lungs."

Mattie laughed and swatted Elaine's arm. "You'll do no such thing. Kristi and I will sit on either side of you and make sure you behave."

"The judging hasn't started yet, has it?" Kristi asked, eyeing the judges' table where Mama Rizzoli sat with her fellow judges, Silvi Kuhlman and Herman Studebakker.

"No. You're just in time," Elaine said, pulling Kristi and Mattie into their seats. "The volunteers just finished setting up the table with the entries."

Kristi scanned the table where the jars to be judged sat in neat rows. Three women were in attendance, an older woman with iron gray curls, a pretty young girl who didn't look old enough to be helping, and a woman close to Kristi's own age wearing navy slacks with a nice, crisp crease, a baby blue cotton shell, and what looked like very comfortable black shoes with almost no heel.

Nudging Elaine, she pointed at the women and asked, "So who are they?"

After a quick glance, Elaine said, "They're the volunteers who help the judges for the canning division." She waved a hand in the air. "You know, making sure the judges have everything they need, like enough water for palate cleansing or a new pen if one runs out of ink, that sort of thing. They also present the pickles and keep track of which jar is which.

"The older woman is Rhonda Gervais. She entered pickles for years, but stopped competing a couple of years ago. The teenager is her granddaughter, Jaci Evans. Rhonda is hoping Jaci will get excited and decide she wants to compete in future fairs. The other lady is Delilah Robinson. She enters baked goods every year, but canning isn't her thing. She never enters pickles... or anything else in this division."

Kristi nodded. "Gotcha. Thanks."

Elaine gave a small squeal and grabbed Kristi's arm. "They're starting! See? Jaci is presenting the first jar!"

"Presenting the first jar?" Kristi asked. "I thought the judges would be tasting the pickles."

Elaine nodded, but kept her gaze glued to the judges' table. "They will, but first they have to inspect the jar for clarity of the liquid, uniformity of the size of the pickles, that all of the pickles are covered with liquid, and that the headspace is correct."

Kristi's mouth dropped open. She closed it quickly before asking, "Seriously? All that before they even taste the pickles?"

Elaine nodded vigorously, but studied the judges' table as the first jar was delivered.

Mattie leaned forward and caught Kristi's eye. "I think I'll stick to quilting," she said in a loud whisper.

Kristi nodded. "You and me both!"

"Shhh." Elaine flapped her hands at her friends. "I want to learn all I can from the judges' reactions to the other entries."

Mattie grinned at Kristi, but leaned back in her seat. The two quilters watched the progress of the judging in silence.

After each judge had inspected the jar and scribbled notes on a sheet of paper Rhonda Gervais provided, Delilah Robinson opened the jar— in full view of the spectators and judges, used a fork to remove a single pickle, and then carefully sliced it into six equal pieces. The pieces were then placed on three small plastic plates and presented to the judges, each with a disposable fork.

The judges waited until they all had their plates, then carefully nibbled on a piece of pickle.

Elaine held her breath, watching their reactions carefully even though Kristi was absolutely positive the current pickles under examination were not Elaine's.

After another bite, and a swallow of water, the judges turned their attention to filling out the paperwork. When all three sat back with their hands in their laps, Herman nodded to a volunteer and their table was cleared.

The same process was followed for six more jars. Kristi was starting to fidget. She wasn't invested in the results like Elaine, and watching three people silently study jars and bite into pickles was actually pretty boring.

Until Jaci picked up the eighth jar.

Suddenly Kristi was acutely aware of the proceedings, with no desire to squirm. Elaine was squeezing her hand so hard she could actually feel her bones grinding together.

"It's mine," Elaine said in a loud stage whisper. "My *dill delights* are up!"

Kristi eased her hand from Elaine's death grip and patted her friend's arm. "They'll love them," she said quietly. "How could they not? Your pickles are delicious."

This time, the procedure was fascinating. Kristi watched with almost as much interest as did Elaine. The unopened jar was examined carefully. The volunteer, Rhonda this time, selected a single pickle and made the cuts. The slices were distributed to the judges. Everything was moving flawlessly. To Kristi's eye, Elaine's pickles were receiving high marks...

...until the judges bit into their slices.

Before they could take a second taste, all three judges blanched. Mama and Silvi covered their mouths with their hands, stood, and collapsed, retching over the edge of the stage.

But not Herman.

Herman turned a putrid shade of green, grabbed his chest, and simply slid off his chair onto the floor of the wooden stage. He didn't move. Didn't groan. Didn't retch. The man was absolutely still.

The volunteers and spectators froze. No one rushed the judges' aid, everyone simply stood or sat in stunned silence.

Until the teenager, Jaci Evans, screamed!

Kristi was the first to recover. She reached across Elaine, grabbed Mattie's hand and said, "Call for the ambulance." All the exhibitors had been briefed on how to get emergency care in case a customer collapsed. "I'll call Jason."

Mattie nodded, whipped out her cell phone, and made the call. Kristi grabbed her own phone, dialed Jason, and caught a volunteer, Delilah, while she waited for the connection. "Don't let anyone leave the area."

Jason's voice sounded calm and cheerful when he answered. "Sheriff Reynolds."

"Jason," Kristi almost shouted, "it's me. We need you in the food court. Hurry."

"What part? It's a big building."

"Judging area for pickles," she said, trying to keep the adrenaline out of her voice. "All three judges collapsed." She lowered her voice. "I think Herman Studebakker might be dead."

"On my way. I'll call for the med techs."

"Mattie already did that. Just hurry."

Ending the call, Kristi stood and faced the onlookers. "Sheriff Reynolds is on his way," she said loudly, but calmly, "and we've called for medical assistance. If everyone would please take your seats, I'm sure the sheriff will want to ask you a few questions about what you might have seen."

She glanced at the judges' table and saw a Delilah starting to clean up. She hurried forward and caught the woman's attention. "Stop. Don't touch anything. Not until the sheriff clears the area."

The woman froze, stared at Kristi, then nodded. "What about the... sick? Shouldn't we clean up that mess?"

"No. Just sit down and wait."

Elaine was white as a sheet. "Those were my pickles," she said, her voice high and thready. She turned glassy eyes on Kristi. "My pickles were the eighth in line!"

Kristi knelt in front of her friend. "Jason will figure everything out, Elaine. Try to stay calm." She glanced at Mattie and said quietly, "Stay with her. I want to check on Mama and Silvi."

Mattie nodded and put her arm around Elaine. "Kristi's right," she murmured to her friend. "Jason will find out what happened. And I'm sure it had nothing to do with your pickles."

Having seen to Elaine, Kristi rounded the stage to check on Mama Rizzoli and Silvi Kuhlman. She found the two women lying in fetal positions between the back of the stage and the divider curtains. The more mature woman, the one with graying hair, Rhonda Gervias, hovered over them, unsure of what to do.

Kristi caught her eye and gestured for the woman to join her. "Medical assistance should be arriving any moment. Have you done anything for either of them?"

The woman wrung her hands and shook her head. "I wasn't sure what to do," she said, giving Kristi an imploring look. "I didn't want to make them worse."

Kristi gave her a small smile and patted her arm. "That's probably for the best. I'm Kristi Lundrigan, by the way."

"Rhonda Gervais," the woman said. "I've won this competition so many times that I no longer compete." She turned her gaze on

Kristi, her eyes gleaming with tears. "Nothing like this has ever happened before."

"Sheriff Reynolds is on his way," Kristi said, trying her best to exude calm confidence. "He'll get to the bottom of this."

Rhonda nodded and straightened her shoulders.

"Please make sure the rest of the volunteers stay here," Kristi said. "And don't let them clean anything or move anything from the judges' table. The sheriff will want to see everything."

"I can do that."

Just then the EMTs arrived and Kristi and Rhonda moved away to give them room to work. Kristi had just rejoined Mattie and Elaine when Jason strode up to them.

The man looked calm and professional in his khaki uniform shirt, blue jeans, cowboy boots, and Stetson hat. His expression was grim as he took in the scene.

"What happened?" he asked Kristi.

"The three judges tasted the batch of pickles and kind of… froze… for a moment. Then Mama Rizzoli and Silvi Kuhlman started vomiting over the edge of the stage."

Jason glanced at the stage where Herman Studebakker's body still lay motionless, an EMT in attendance. "What about Herman? Did he vomit too?"

Kristi shook her head. "No. His complexion turned an odd shade and he grabbed his chest. Then he just slid off his chair and landed on the floor."

While they were talking, three deputies arrived and converged on Jason, led by Janet Millson, Jason's second in command.

"How do you want us to handle this, Sheriff?" Deputy Millson asked after Jason briefed his officers.

"Make sure no one leaves, cordon off the judges' table and the table with the jars, and then start taking statements." He paused, glanced at Kristi, and said, "I'll take care of Kristi and her two friends, then I'll speak to the EMTs."

The deputies all nodded and moved away, Deputy Millson dividing up the tasks.

Jason turned back to Kristi and her friends. "Do you happen to know whose pickles caused the problem?"

Mattie and Kristi shuffled their feet and avoided Jason's gaze, but Elaine raised her hand.

"Th-they were m-mine," she said, her voice hitching. "Th-they were j-judging *my* p-pickles!"

9

SATURDAY AFTERNOON

Kristi left Elaine in Mattie's care while she shadowed Jason, staying close enough to hear what he was saying, but not close enough to cause him to dismiss her. Once he'd finished questioning Elaine about her pickles, he went in search of the fair official in charge of the entire food division. When he found her, he informed her was shutting down *all* of the competitions involving food.

Several other fair officials joined the conversation, having been alerted by the ambulances and law enforcement vehicles parked outside the building that housed all of the food related competitions. They were in a tizzy, but couldn't disagree that Sheriff Reynolds was being proactive about guarding the public's safety.

"We're going to have a lot of upset contestants," one official told him, waving her arm to indicate all the divisions of pies, cakes, and breads, as well as the jams and jellies, dried fruit, and canned goods. "Not only will we miss giving out ribbons, but we'll lose income! We won't be able to auction off the entries! This is a disaster!"

Jason listened patiently. When she wound down, he said, "May I remind you that you have one dead judge and two others in need of hospitalization?" The woman had the grace to lower her eyes, her face blushing a rosy pink. "The food department is closed," Jason continued. "Period. I won't stand by and take a chance on another poisoning."

She sighed and nodded. "You're right, of course, Sheriff." She glanced up at him, eyes glistening with tears. "It's just that everyone has worked so hard for this event. But..." she straightened her shoulders and lifted her chin, "circumstances have changed. I'll have all of the contestants gather their entries and take them home."

"No," Jason said emphatically. "You won't. We'll be taking everything into evidence."

The woman looked shocked. "Everything? But the pies and cakes have nothing to do with dill pickles!"

"True," he said, nodding. "But we don't know that the pickles were the only food item targeted. Just alert your people that the events are closed and that my department will be contacting them to take their statements. Oh, and you'll need to provide us with a list of all contestants, volunteers, and crew. Anyone who at anytime dealt with the food divisions."

She gulped, looked a bit pale, then straightened her shoulders again. "Of course, Sheriff. Whatever you need." After a moment's hesitation, she asked, "What about the vendors in the food court? Will you be shutting them down as well?"

He knew she was thinking of even greater lost revenue... of all the fair-goers who wouldn't be able to buy lunches and snacks, but he shook his head.

"No," he said. "That won't be necessary. We have business licenses and contact information on those vendors already. As long as we don't have a rash of food poisoning stemming from fair food, they're good to go. But all your exhibits will be off limits to the public."

She nodded and turned to gather her workers and carry out his orders.

Kristi, who had been eavesdropping on his conversation while keeping an eye on Elaine, approached Jason.

"Your department has a lot of work ahead of them," she said quietly. "There must be hundreds of entries in the food divisions."

He pulled his Stetson off and wiped his forehead on his sleeve before nodding. "Too much for us to deal with. I've called in the State crime scene people. They have the manpower and the labs to determine exactly what's going on and how widespread it is."

He replaced his hat, took her arm, and guided her to a quieter area. "Closing everything down is undoubtedly overkill, but I just can't take the chance. If one of those judges was the intended target, then we can't know that pickles were the only tainted food. After all, each of them was judging several divisions."

Kristi shivered and stared around the building, taking in all of the various types of food that had been assembled for the contests. After a quick glance at Elaine, she turned her attention back to Jason.

"You don't really think Elaine did this, do you?"

He released the breath he'd been holding, and took her hand. "I sincerely hope not. I like Elaine, and I know you're close to her, but right now, she's our prime suspect." He paused, made eye contact and held her gaze. "You know I'm going to have to arrest her."

Kristi yanked her hand from his, indignation flaring, ready to defend her friend. But before she could speak, he continued, "It's procedure, Kristi. No one is going to browbeat her or try to force her to confess, but until we know what's going on, she's going to be detained."

Kristi deflated. Jason knew his job and did it well. He'd get to the bottom of this mess. She just had to trust him.

"What can I do?"

"If you can leave your booth, I'd like you to come with us to the station. She'll be calmer with a friendly face." He smiled at her. "And it's not like I think Elaine is a hardened criminal."

"Definitely not." Kristi took a deep breath, considered her options, and walked over to join Mattie and Elaine.

"Mattie," she said quietly, "I'd like to speak to you... privately."

The two women moved away from Elaine, who sat with her head in her hands, seemingly oblivious to the activity around her.

"What's happening?" Mattie asked, her gaze still on Elaine.

"I need you to help Eula man the booth for the rest of the day. Are you up to that?"

Mattie cocked her head and raised an eyebrow, but nodded. "Yes. Of course. Where will you be?"

Kristi sighed and placed a hand on Mattie's shoulder. "Jason wants me to accompany Elaine when he takes her in to the station."

Mattie's face paled and her eyes widened. "He's arresting her?"

Kristi nodded. "He doesn't think she's guilty, but he has to take her in. He thinks she'll feel safer if I'm there."

Mattie closed her eyes and nodded. "Just promise me you'll make sure she has a lawyer if she needs one."

"Trust me, I won't let anyone, not even Jason, take advantage of her." Kristi paused for a moment before continuing, "Are you sure you're up to helping Eula? I can call Andrea in if you need to go home."

"I'll be fine," Mattie said with a weak smile. "Just take care of Elaine. And call me when you know anything."

"Count on it."

The two women rejoined Elaine, where Mattie explained that she had to get back to work, but that Kristi would stay with Elaine as moral support. Hugging her friend quickly, Mattie hurried off to the vendors' exhibition building.

As soon as she was gone, Elaine looked up at Kristi with a tremulous smile. "Thanks for sticking with me."

"No problem. If you'd rather, I can trade places with Mattie..."

Elaine shook her head. "No. I think it's better if you hold my hand through this." Tears shone in her eyes. "It's too reminiscent of what Mattie went through when Gary was murdered."

Kristi nodded and settled into the folding chair beside her. "You're a good friend, Elaine." Placing an arm around Elaine's shoulders, Kristi gave her a gentle hug. "Everything will work out."

Nodding, Elaine glanced up at the judges' table, which was currently unattended, but would soon be teeming with officials since the state crime scene investigators had just arrived. They were setting up their equipment and boxes to collect evidence between the judges' table and the table holding the jars of pickles yet to be judged.

Elaine frowned and cocked her head. They were sitting in the first row of spectator seats and had a clear view of the judges' table. Suddenly, she stood, though she made no move to approach the table.

"Kristi," she hissed. "There's something wrong."

Biting her tongue to keep from saying, *Well duh! A man's been murdered!* Kristi stood and instead asked, "What? What are you looking at, Elaine?"

"I was so nervous about the judging, I didn't even notice before."

"What?"

"Those aren't my pickles!"

Kristi stared at her friend, then glanced at the open jar on the table. It looked like all the other jars of pickles to her. Small green pickled cucumbers covered in liquid, with sprigs of dill weed jammed between the cukes. What did Elaine see that Kristi didn't?

"How can you tell?"

Elaine turned to Kristi, grabbed her hands, and practically

bounced up and down in excitement. "Look at the jar! That's not one of mine. That's an old-fashioned square jar. My mom used to use them, but you can't buy them anymore... at least not readily." She squeezed Kristi's hands, relief etching her face. "All of my canning jars are the standard round kind!"

10

SATURDAY EVENING

Kristi dragged herself through the kitchen door that evening, almost too tired to walk. The day had been more emotionally draining than she could have imagined when she left home that morning.

Stitches and Between, as though understanding her exhaustion, sat quietly watching as she hung her denim shoulder bag and keys on their respective hooks by the door. They followed her to the living room, and when she collapsed on the couch, they jumped up on either side of her and snuggled against her legs, purring loudly.

"Thanks, kitty-kids," she said, stroking them both. Good thing she had two hands! "And thanks for not winding around my legs when I came in the door. I'm not sure I wouldn't have fallen over."

She leaned her head back, closed her eyes, and allowed the cats' purring contentment to wash over her. The afternoon had turned out better than she'd feared when she'd first agreed to accompany Jason and Elaine to the station, but it had still been an ordeal... and she hadn't even been the one being arrested!

Kristi had made sure Elaine pointed out the difference in the canning jars to Jason before they left the scene of the crime. Good thing too, since that turned out to be a key piece of evidence. One that someone unfamiliar with canning might overlook.

Jason had immediately sent one of his deputies to Elaine's home, both to alert her husband and to inventory her canning supplies. By the time Jason, Kristi, and Elaine arrived at the station, Vic Hastings had already arrived... with the deputy in tow.

"Sheriff Reynolds," Vic said the instant he saw Jason, "I don't know what you think you're doing, but my wife wouldn't poison anybody." He rushed to Elaine's side and put his arms around her, though his angry gaze remained firmly on Jason. "First, she wouldn't know how, and second, she wouldn't have any reason to. Why are you focused on Elaine?"

Jason removed his Stetson, wiped his forehead on his sleeve, and motioned Vic and Elaine to his office. "Let's talk in there, it's quieter."

Kristi followed the other three, then stood against the wall while Vic and Elaine took the visitor chairs opposite Jason's battered, old-fashioned school teacher's desk. Jason glanced at her, noted that she was standing, and lifted the receiver of his desk phone to ask a deputy to bring in an extra chair.

When the deputy brought the chair— which made the small office feel really crowded— the man paused and cleared his throat.

"What is it, Lawson?" Jason asked, placing his Stetson on top of a file cabinet and pulling out his desk chair.

"Well, sir," Lawson said, "I just wondered if you wanted me to tell you about Mrs. Hasting's canning stuff now, or wait 'til later?"

A slight frown marred Jason's handsome face as he considered a moment before deciding. "What did you find?"

Deputy Lawson pulled a small notebook from his back pocket

and flipped it open. "I'll type the whole list up for you, but the important parts are that I didn't find anything that appeared to be poisonous in nature— I'll be more certain of that once the coroner tells us what we're looking for— and, just like Mrs. Hastings reported, all of her canning jars, no matter the size, were round. She didn't have a single squared-off jar in the house."

Jason nodded. "Thanks, Lawson. Appreciate your good work."

Deputy Lawson nodded, stepped out of the office, and closed the door behind himself.

"Well," Jason said, slapping the top of his desk with both hands, "that sure makes things easier." He held up one of those hands to forestall Vic's retort. "Take it easy, Vic. I don't think Elaine killed anyone, but procedures have to be followed, and it certainly appeared that Elaine's pickles were the ones being tasted when the judges all collapsed."

Elaine patted her husband's hand. "That's true, Vic. *I* even thought they were judging my pickles until I noticed the jar... and that wasn't until after the ambulance had taken all the judges away! Don't be mad at the sheriff; he's been nothing but kind to me." She nodded toward Kristi. "Why he even had Kristi come along so I wouldn't be alone here at the station."

Vic's shoulders relaxed and his face lost some of its redness. After a moment, he nodded. "Apologies, Sheriff. I may have overreacted."

Jason waved the comment away. "Not to worry. It's not everyday a man's wife is taken into custody." He turned his attention to Elaine. "Since the jar doesn't match anything in your supplies and I don't have a motive tying you to this, I'm going to release you on your own recognizance, Elaine. But I will caution you not to leave the area. Go home, get some rest, and think about the events of the judging. Maybe write out your thoughts, if that helps. If you think of anything that happened that seems, in hindsight, significant... out of the ordinary... let me know right away."

"Of course, Sheriff," Elaine said after sighing loudly. "I'll write down everything I can think of before I go to bed tonight." She jumped up, rushed over to Kristi and pulled her friend up into a tight hug. "Thank you so much for staying with me through this," she whispered. "I'll never forget it!"

Kristi hugged her just as tightly. "Of course. I'm just sorry you've had to be involved in this. But Jason will find the real culprit." She held Elaine at arm's length and locked gazes with her. "He's very good at what he does!"

A moment later, Vic and Elaine had disappeared from the office. Jason gave a wry chuckle. "Doesn't take people long to leave once they're released, does it?"

He walked around his desk and put an arm around Kristi. "Thanks for your help today. You and Mattie kept Elaine calm."

Kristi started to protest that she hadn't done anything, but Jason shook his head. "If you hadn't been there to support her, she might not have calmed down enough for the difference in the jars to register." He stared out of the office door, as if he could still see the departing couple. "I'd hate to have had to keep Elaine locked up in a cell overnight just because of a missed detail."

"You're convinced she had nothing to do with this, aren't you?" Kristi asked, cocking her head and giving him a sidelong glance.

"I am, but I've got no proof one way or the other." He sighed and stepped back around his desk. "I sure hope the coroner and the crime lab come up with some facts." He studied her for a moment. "Are you okay to drive home, or would you like one of my deputies to give you a lift?"

"I'm fine," she said with a wave of her hand, "and everyone here is busy. Will I see you tomorrow?"

He nodded. "It may only be for a moment or two at the fair, but I'll make a point of dropping by the booth."

"I'll look forward to it."

...and she was, but right now, she needed to find her feet,

shuffle into the kitchen and feed herself and her cats. Giving Stitches and Between a final rub, Kristi pushed herself upright and strode toward the kitchen.

"Come on, kitty-kids," she called to her two little emotional support cats. "Let's fix dinner." Not needing to hear that magic word twice, both cats leapt from the couch and raced Kristi to the cabinet where their food was kept.

"You two deserve a reward for taking such good care of me this evening," she said, opening an upper cabinet and choosing a can of white albacore tuna. As if in agreement, Stitches rubbed against one of Kristi's legs, while Between wound himself around her other ankle. At the sound of the electric can opener, both cats froze and stared up at the can in Kristi's hand.

The delicious aroma of tuna wafted through the room, and Kristi laughed softly at the rapt expression on both cats' faces.

"Nothing but the best for my favorite kitty-kids," she murmured as she divided the tuna between two saucers, placed them on the floor, and filled their bowls with dry kibble.

Now that the cats were cared for, Kristi turned to the refrigerator to contemplate her own meal. The first thing she saw was a large jar of dill pickles.

"Absolutely not!"

Closing the refrigerator, she opened the freezer compartment instead. She'd cook tomorrow. Tonight, she'd make do with a frozen dinner.

Meatloaf and mashed potatoes. She nodded to herself as she placed the meal in the microwave and hit the start button. Just what she needed.

Not a cucumber or bit of dill weed in sight!

11

SUNDAY MORNING

The next morning Kristi drove to the fairgrounds bright and early, relieved that she only had one venue to worry about today. Since *Delectable Mountain Quilting* was always closed on Sundays, the booth at the fair was her only point of sale for the day. She was also glad that Mattie, along with Ruby and Eula, had the day off. Mattie had confided in Kristi during a phone call last night that she planned to spend today with Elaine and Vic.

Kristi sighed. A day together would be good for both of her friends.

Turning onto the fairgrounds, Kristi pulled into the exhibitor's parking lot right behind an older, dusty, blue Jeep Cherokee. She parked beside the vehicle and when she stepped out of her red Subaru Outback was pleased to see Andrea Jansson, one of her temporary employees, emerging from the Jeep. Much like Kristi, the young woman was dressed for work, wearing slim khaki pants, a dark green cotton tee-shirt, and comfortable brown running shoes. Kristi's ensemble included navy blue pants, pale blue silk shell, and, of course, her quilter's chatelaine.

"Good morning, Andrea," she called to her temporary clerk, "Are you ready for a day at the fair?"

"Sure am," Andrea said with a grin.

Kristi knew how lucky she was that Andrea had come home from her community college in Billings for the summer... and that she'd been willing to work for *Delectable Mountain Quilting* during fair week! Andrea was an effervescent young woman with a sparkling personality. She could easily have found summer work in the city. Fortunately for Kristi, Andrea had missed her family and longed to return to the ranch.

Tall and lean, with dark brown hair and hazel eyes, Andrea was as much at home in the saddle as she was in the quilt shop. She'd been riding since she was a toddler and had been sewing bits of fabric together almost as long. Ranch families worked hard, and their little ones learned to lend a hand early.

Kristi and Andrea showed their exhibitor badges to the guard at the entrance and made their way to their booth.

"I sure hope today is more like Friday than like yesterday," Kristi said as she stowed her embroidered denim shoulder bag under a table.

"I heard about the mess at the pickle judging," Andrea said, placing her dark leather backpack beside Kristi's bag. "Did they really close *all* the food competitions?"

Kristi nodded. "A man died, after all."

"That's unreal. My mom has entered almost every food division over the years and we've never heard of anything like that happening before. Why, my sister Becca and I used to enter brownies and such in the junior division when we were kids." She shook her head sadly. "I can't imagine!"

"Did your mom enter this year?"

Andrea nodded. "She had a peach pie in pastries." She paused to straighten a bolt of fabric before continuing, "Can you believe it? Her pie is at the lab right now. They're probably testing it for poison as we speak."

"I sure hope they find out what happened, and fast. It was awful. Seeing Mama Rizzoli and Silvi Kuhlman keel over sick like that. And Herman Studebakker..." Kristi shivered.

Andrea's eye widened. "Were you there?"

Kristi nodded. "Mattie and I went to support our friend Elaine. Her pickles were being judged."

"I'm so sorry, Kristi. I hadn't realized you actually saw what happened. How terrible!"

"It was pretty horrible." Kristi straightened her shoulders and made an effort to smile. "But let's put those thoughts away for now. We want to be upbeat for our customers."

But putting it away was easier said than done. Almost everyone who visited the booth that morning was buzzing about yesterday's scandal at the food building.

"I heard one of the pickle makers pulled out a gun and threatened everyone! Even the spectators!" The speaker, a woman in her forties with her hair dyed purple, turned to Kristi. "Aren't you afraid to have a booth in this fair?"

Kristi smiled and shook her head. "First, there were no guns at the pickle judging. Second, I'm sure the sheriff has everything under control."

"Besides," Andrea said, scooping up a pile of fabric bolts to reshelve them, "you're here, aren't you? How worried can you be?" She flashed such an innocent expression at the purple-haired woman that Kristi had hard time keeping a straight face.

The booth had a lull mid-morning and Kristi shooed Andrea off on her break. The college girl grabbed her backpack and disappeared into the crowd, anxious to see what the rest of the exhibitor building held.

Kristi had just settled in a chair with a bottle of water when Deputy Millson strode into the booth.

"Morning, Ms. Lundrigan," the young woman said, tipping her Stetson to Kristi. Janet Millson was a good-looking woman, with a rich coppery complexion and dark eyes that gleamed with intelligence. As usual, her thick black hair was pulled into a tight knot at the back of her neck, while her official khaki shirt and pants were clean and pressed.

Kristi gestured to the chair Andrea had so recently vacated. "Have a seat, Deputy and tell me what I can do for you." She cocked her head and studied Jason's second in command. "You haven't decided to take up quilting, have you?"

Janet Millson grinned and sat. "Nope. Sheriff Reynolds asked me to stop by and bring you up to speed on the investigation."

"Really?" Kristi leaned forward, eager to hear what the deputy had to say. "What have you learned?"

"Well, the main thing is the report came in from the lab in Billings." Deputy Millson glanced around as if to ensure that they were still alone. She lowered her voice. "That wasn't dill weed in that jar of pickles."

Kristi frowned. "It wasn't? What was it?"

"Hemlock."

Kristi gasped. Having grown up in Montana, Kristi knew that hemlock grew wild and that the pernicious weed could be mistaken for dill, but who in their right mind would risk harvesting wild dill for pickles they intended to enter in the fair?

"Does Jason think it was an accident? Someone used hemlock instead of dill by mistake?"

Janet shook her head. "Nope, and neither do I." She leaned even closer to Kristi. "Here's the thing, the jar with the tainted pickles? It wasn't even an official entry. We found Ms. Hasting's jar of pickles hidden under a table."

"But," Kristi leaned back, her eyes wide, "who would do such a thing? And how can you be sure which jar of pickles was which?"

"We can be sure. All the entrants' jars were marked with coded stickers on the bottom of the jars where they couldn't be seen by the judges. The tainted jar wasn't marked."

"But then," Kristi said, frowning, "how did the tainted jar end up on the judges' table?"

Deputy Millson tilted her head and tapped her nose. "That's the question, isn't it?" After a moment, she stood and touched the brim of her hat in salute. "Anyway, Sheriff Reynolds thought you'd want to know that Ms. Hastings has moved way down our list of suspects."

Kristi rose and followed the deputy to the aisle, which was still teeming with fair-goers. "That's true," she said. "Thanks for taking the time to let me know."

"No problem," Deputy Millson said, and then melted into the crowded walkway.

SUNDAY AFTERNOON

Later that afternoon, Kristi left Andrea in charge of the booth and took a much needed break.

"Are you sure you're comfortable with me leaving for a bit?" Kristi asked the young woman.

Andrea flapped her hands toward the main walkway. The aisle was much less crowded than it had been that morning, and the booth was currently deserted except for the two of them. "Go. Find something interesting to look at. I'll be fine."

"Okay. If you're sure. I really did want to see how the judging in the quilt show turned out."

"Go," Andrea repeated. "Have fun!"

Smiling, Kristi grabbed her embroidered shoulder bag and headed to the building next door. Like the exhibitor's building, this much smaller hall was a single large room divided into sections by moveable partitions. This year it was divided into three parts: photographic and fine arts, home arts, and floral arrangements.

Quilts were included in home arts, along with other sewing projects, spinning, weaving, wood carving, decorative painting, and leather craft. Kristi had intended to do a thorough walk-through of the building yesterday, but.... Well, Elaine's difficulties had taken precedence. She didn't want to take the time to look at everything today, not while Andrea was alone in the booth, so she hurried past some intriguing art works and made straight for the quilt show.

The quilts hung from suspended rods and were grouped by division: hand pieced; machine pieced; appliqué; and whole cloth. Each division was further broken down. Hand pieced quilts could be antique or contemporary, sized for a wall hanging, a bed, or a baby. Machine pieced might be regular or paper-pieced, and in wall, bed, or crib size. And whole cloth quilts were just what they sounded like—no piecing involved, but the quilting patterns (whether by hand or machine) could be extraordinary.

She wandered through the beautiful examples of other women's work until she reached the antique hand pieced quilts. Kristi had entered Nanna Van Oss's 1930s Pickle Dish quilt and was delighted to see that her grandmother's work had been awarded third place. She would display that yellow ribbon with pride... probably in the shop, possibly with the quilt itself. At least for a little while.

Seeking out the other winners, she was thrilled to see that the blue ribbon had gone to a Double Wedding Ring quilt belonging to the Marsten family. Kristi had done an appraisal of Mrs. Marsten's quilt collection last year and had greatly admired this 1870s quilt. She was glad to know that her customer, Anna Marsten, had convinced her mother-in-law to enter it in the fair.

The staff of *Delectable Mountain Quilting* had also done well in the show. Eula Gibbs' hand pieced Irish Chain baby quilt won a blue ribbon, while Mattie Stebbings' beautiful machine pieced Delectable Mountain quilt took second place for a red ribbon in the bed quilt section. Ruby Andrews entered a lovely paper-pieced wall quilt of a violet growing against a brick wall, and though she hadn't gotten a ribbon, Kristi heard lots of nice comments about the little quilt in the short time she was there.

Kristi smiled as she walked through the show and enjoyed the bright colors and inventive designs. Her shop might see an uptick in customers in the coming weeks as current quilters were inspired to try new patterns, and novices sought classes to learn the traditional art.

Yes, between the quilt show and the booth, the Garnet County Fair was going to be *very* good for business!

Later that afternoon, Kristi did another demonstration on how to piece a Pickle Dish block by machine. This demo was even more fun than the first one, since she could now tell her audience about the yellow ribbon awarded to her grandmother's hand pieced Pickle Dish quilt. She encouraged all her listeners to head over to the quilt show and be inspired by the many beautiful quilts... and to take a look at the finished Pickle Dish. After all, she planned to teach a class on its construction in the fall!

After the demo, the booth had a lull in traffic, so Kristi insisted that Andrea take a nice long break.

"Go," Kristi said. "Enjoy the fair. Maybe check out the quilt show. You've been hard at it all day, and, except for that break this morning, you haven't left the booth. You even ate lunch here."

"Hey. I came prepared with my own lunch, but thanks," Andrea said, grabbing her backpack from its hiding place under a table. "I could use a break, and after watching your demo, I really want to see a finished Pickle Dish. That's a pattern I've never seen made up."

Kristi nodded. "It's not as well known as some, but Nanna did her quilt in the traditional colors, white and green with red accents. It's a beauty, if I do say so myself."

"Can't wait to see it." Andrea waved as she moved into the aisle. "Bye!"

Alone at last— in a crowd of fair-goers— Kristi slumped into a chair, pulled out a bottle of water and drank deeply. The day had gone well. Much better than she'd expected, actually. Sure there had been quite a few people gossiping about the murder in the canning section, but no one had named Elaine as a suspect, so Kristi had let the rumors flow over her. She shivered again, remembering Janet Millson's report that the judges had been poisoned with hemlock. Who in their right mind would season pickles with wild hemlock?

No one. Which was why the deputy didn't think the poisoning was an accident.

But which of the judges was the intended victim? Surely not all of them! Kristi frowned. The tainted pickles made Mama Rizzoli and Silvi Kuhlman ill… but they killed Herman Studebakker. Was that intentional, or did something else make the poison affect Herman more severely?

Did the culprit intend to kill? Or just disrupt the judging?

And how did that tainted jar end up on the judges' table?

So many questions!

At least Elaine was no longer the primary suspect. But Kristi knew it would take a long time before her friend would be able to open a jar of her *dill delights* without remembering Herman Studebakker's untimely death.

SUNDAY EVENING

Kristi was packing up for the evening, having sent Andrea home already, when Jason walked into the booth.

"Finished for the day?" he asked.

"Yep," she said, "and ready to head home and put my feet up."

"Ah," he said, looking a little crestfallen. "Then I guess you wouldn't be interested in going out to dinner."

"Nope," she said, pulling her embroidered denim shoulder bag from beneath the table. She turned to him and grinned. "But I'd love to have pizza and a movie with you. Want to come over? We'll order your favorite pizza, Canadian bacon and black olive, and see what movies are streaming."

He laughed. "You've got a date! Come on. I'll follow you home."

Forty-five minutes later Kristi and Jason relaxed in her living room, her in the corner of her forest green couch and him in the beige recliner that sat beside her rarely used fireplace. Stitches sprawled on the cushion beside Kristi, while Between stalked Jason's Stetson.

The sheriff pointed his finger at the little tuxedo cat and said in his sternest voice, "Don't even think about it."

Between promptly dropped to his haunches and began grooming his tail as if he'd had nothing else in mind all along.

Kristi smothered a laugh and gestured toward the pizza box that rested on the coffee table between them. "Now that you have my cat under control, grab another slice."

"Well, if you insist," he said with a grin and plopped another piece of cheesy, tomatoey goodness onto his paper plate. He exhaled a contented sigh. "Fine dining at its best!"

Kristi bit off a piece of crust and chewed thoughtfully. This was almost like old times. Back in their married days, when she'd expected to spend the rest of her life with this man. She peeked at Jason as he ate his slice of pizza, head resting on the back of her recliner, eyes half-closed as he relaxed.

What did she expect out of this second-chance relationship?

They'd been dating for more than a year now with nothing more than a few kisses. Neither of them wanted to rush things and risk damaging their chances, but chances at what? Did she think they'd marry again? Did he?

She knew she loved him. Doubted she'd ever love anyone else. But did that mean she wanted to commit to him again? Risk being betrayed by him again?

She grabbed her glass of iced tea and sipped before taking another bite of pizza.

What was she worrying about? She didn't even know if Jason was thinking of marriage. Though they'd enjoyed a very satisfying sex life during their marriage, he hadn't made any overtures toward spending the night in all this time. Fourteen months, and the man hadn't once tried to sleep with her!

Of course, she hadn't asked him to stay either.

They'd been very careful of their relationship. Maybe too careful.

Jason leaned forward and snagged another slice. He met her gaze and said, "You're very quiet. What are you thinking about?"

Kristi felt her cheeks heat. Should she tell him? She studied the remains of the pizza on her paper plate and considered lying, telling him she was thinking about the murder. But what good would that do either of them?

She was an adult. So was he. Either they could talk to each other or...

...or they had no future together.

She raised her eyes and met his gaze. "I was thinking about us," she said quietly. "About our relationship, and what we want out of it."

He nodded, setting his plate aside. "I've been thinking about that a lot lately." He glanced around the room, gestured to her and the cats. "This is very comfortable. It feels right." He captured her gaze. "What do you think? Have we been moving slow long enough?"

She bit her lip, then nodded. "I think so. What do you see happening next?"

He stood and moved to the couch, picked up Stitches and dumped her on the floor. "Sorry, Kitty-kid. You're in my spot." He sat beside Kristi, pulled her into his arms and kissed her passionately.

"I've been biding my time," he whispered as he nuzzled her ear. "Waiting for you to give me a signal that you were ready." He nipped her lower lip, then leaned back to study her. "Are you ready?"

Kristi melted. Fire raged through her system, consuming her thoughts and her senses.

This. This was what she wanted. She wanted Jason. In her bed. In her body. She wanted the closeness and intimacy they'd always shared.

And she wanted it now.

"I'm ready," she said, her voice husky with desire. Right now, she didn't care where this might lead. Right now, she just wanted Jason.

Jason didn't need any further encouragement. He picked her

up, kissed her thoroughly, and carried her to the bedroom. Placing her carefully on the bed, he laid down beside her and pulled her close, kissing her thoroughly.

Kristi opened her lips, accepting his tongue, and reached for the buttons on his shirt. She wanted to touch him, to feel the warmth of his skin beneath her fingers. She'd just managed the run her hands over his bare chest and wrap her arms around him beneath his shirt when his cell phone beeped.

He broke their kiss, leaned back and frowned.

"Ignore it," she said and kissed his neck.

He rested his forehead against hers. "I can't. That's my official tone." He rolled away from her, pulled the cell phone from its case on his belt, and answered.

"Sheriff Reynolds," he said, his voice gruff with irritation. He listened for a few moments, nodded though the person on the other end couldn't see him, and said, "I'll be right there."

He ended the call and turned to Kristi. "I'm sorry…"

"Don't be," she said, sitting up. "I'm well aware that this is who you are." She smiled, though it was a bit tremulous. "Rain check?"

He pulled her into his arms and kissed her again. "You better believe it," he said gruffly. "Woe be to my deputies if this turns out to be nothing." He stood, buttoned his shirt and retucked it. "I'll call you."

"I'll be waiting."

As he strode to the bedroom door, she called his name.

"Jason!"

He paused, looking back over his shoulder, his eyebrows lifted.

"Be careful," she said.

He nodded. "Always am."

And then he was gone. She heard the front door close and got up to go put the remains of the pizza away. She smiled ruefully as she slid the box into the refrigerator. At least they'd answered one question, he still desired her. Other questions could wait.

But right now? A cold shower was in order!

14

MONDAY MORNING

Kristi stretched languidly when she awoke the next morning. She'd been enjoying the *best* dream. Jason had stayed, and she'd spent the night cuddled in his arms as well as enjoying much more *active* delights. She glanced at the other side of her bed and sighed. No handsome man, unfortunately. Just Stitches and Between. The cats occupied the space where her dream Jason should have been. One cat curled into a tight little ball, the other stretched out like a furry black rope.

If Jason hadn't gotten that call last night, he might have been sleeping there in reality.

She smiled, but pushed at the corners of that thought. How did she feel about that? Would she like waking up next to him again, or would his presence feel like an intrusion into her ordered life?

After a moment's consideration, she laughed and jumped from the bed. Intrusion? Not hardly! She couldn't wait to share her life and her bed with Jason again! Her kitty-kids might find his presence intrusive, but they'd get over it. Kristi loved Jason, had always loved Jason, and dearly hoped that one day they'd be a couple again. In every sense of the word.

Both cats sat up and watched as she raced through her morning routine. When she strode out of the bedroom and headed for the kitchen, they raced ahead, anxious to arrive first, in case she did anything unexpected.

"No worries, kitty-kids," she practically sang. "Nothing's wrong, I'm just happy."

She stopped with her hand on the cabinet door. It was true. She was happy. A man was dead, two women hospitalized, but she, Kristiana Lundrigan, was happy! Closing her eyes, she savored the feeling.

After a moment, she opened her eyes and continued her breakfast preparations. Dry kibble and a slice of hard-boiled egg for the kitty-kids, and granola smothered in peach yogurt for her.

An hour later, Kristi parked her red Subaru Outback in the small, gravel lot behind the shop and unlocked the back door. She paused a moment before stepping inside. Hard to believe that just a little over a year ago she'd found a man's dead body in this very spot. Shaking her head, she entered the combination kitchen / break room and strode to her locker. How long would it have taken, she wondered, for her and Jason to get back together if Gary Stebbings hadn't been murdered on her very doorstep?

Before she could follow that thought down a rabbit hole, the back door opened and Eula Gibbs came in.

"Morning, Kristi," the older woman said in a cheerful voice.

"Good morning to you, too."

"Are you glad to be back in the shop today?" Eula asked.

Kristi nodded. "I am, actually. The booth is doing very well, but the crowds do get a bit tiresome." She glanced around the familiar room, stepping through the doorway onto the sales floor and turning on the lights. The shop— *her* shop— fairly glowed with color, all arranged in a satisfying pallet. She sighed with contentment.

"It'll be restful, I think," she said quietly, "being back in the shop today."

"I agree," Eula said, stashing her purse in her locker. "I enjoyed my day at the fair, but I'm happy to be here in the shop today." She turned to Kristi. "Who's minding the booth today?"

"Mattie and Ruby."

"They'll do great," Eula said.

"They will," Kristi agreed. "Plus, if they get overwhelmed, Mattie has permission to call Andrea in."

Eula cocked her head, frowned, then laughed. "That's great, but you know how the fair ebbs and flows… by the time Andrea arrived, the crush would be over."

"True enough, which is why I doubt Mattie will call her. Still, it's reassuring to know that she can."

With that the two women separated and ran through their opening routine. Kristi checked the cash register and made sure the weekend's receipts were properly filed while Eula checked the supply of fat quarters and made sure that any fabric bolts left near the cutting table were reshelved. When the shop was ready for customers, Kristi flipped the sign to "Open" and unlocked the front door.

The morning was quiet, as Kristi had anticipated. Most of her regular customers were probably at the fair, and any visitors from out of town most definitely were there. She hoped Mattie and Ruby were having a busy, but not *too* busy, morning.

Eula sat in the comfortable overstuffed chair with her chatelaine around her neck and a hand piecing project in her lap. Kristi had added that chair after seeing a few husbands accompany their wives to the store and then stand around looking out of place. She'd placed it near the front window so the men could watch the foot traffic outside while their wives shopped. Comfortable men were less likely to rush their wives, and Kristi wanted her customers to take all the time they needed over their fabric choices.

While Eula pieced, Kristi sat on the stool behind the counter and worked on her laptop. She was busily typing lesson plans for the class on the Pickle Dish quilt when the bell over the front door jingled. She glanced up and smiled as Jason walked in. He touched the brim of his hat in acknowledgement to Eula, but strode straight to Kristi.

"Do you have a minute?" he asked.

"Good morning to you, too," she teased, but immediately sobered. "Of course." Turning to Eula, she said, "I'll be in the back, if you need anything."

"Take your time," Eula said. "I doubt we'll have a stampede in the next few minutes."

Nodding, Kristi crooked her finger and led Jason to the break room.

The moment they were alone, Jason pulled Kristi into his arms. "Sorry about last night," he whispered. "I really wanted to stay."

Kristi wrapped her arms around his waist and leaned her head against his chest. "I really wanted you to stay, too." She listened to the steady beat of his heart and enjoyed the warmth of his arms for a moment more before pushing back and stepping out of his embrace.

"Can you tell me what happened?"

Jason scowled. "Another case of food poisoning. This time at Mama Rizzoli's restaurant."

Kristi gasped. "Did anyone die?"

Jason shook his head. "Not this time."

"W-was it hemlock again?"

"We won't know until we get the lab work back, but it sure looked the same." He pulled off his Stetson, placed it on the table, and scrubbed his face with his hands. "We closed the restaurant and the crime scene techs are scouring the kitchen for poisons."

"Who was poisoned?" Kristi asked, feeling a bit guilty that she hadn't asked immediately.

"Matt Jenkins. He was having dinner with a group of friends, but only his food was tainted."

"Does... does he have a family?" she asked.

"He and his wife divorced years ago. She moved to Atlanta, but his teenage son, Henry, lives with him."

"Oh. Who will look after the boy while Matt is hospitalized?"

Jason smiled. "You planning to adopt the boy?" When she glared at him, he raised his hands in surrender. "Never mind. Poor timing for a joke. Henry will be a senior in the fall. He can take care of himself for a few days."

Kristi nodded, then frowned. "Wait a minute... doesn't Matt work for Herman Studebakker?"

Jason nodded. "Actually, Matt and Herman are... well, were... partners in *The Honey Barrel Brewpub*."

Kristi sat down in one of the chairs at the table. "So last night's poisoning," she said, her brows creased in thought, "is related to the pickle judging twice over... three times if it turns out to be hemlock again. First, it happened at Rizzoli's, and Mama Rizzoli was one of the first victims, then last night's victim is the partner of the man who died in the first poisoning." She shook her head. "I don't know whether that means Mama or Herman was the intended victim the first time around."

"Or whether it means someone related to Mama Rizzoli is our poisoner," Jason finished. He sighed, pulled out a chair, and joined Kristi at the table. "I know. It's more information, but the threads are so tangled, I can't see where they lead."

"It's a puzzle all right." Kristi placed a hand on Jason's arm and waited for him to meet her gaze. "But I have every faith in your ability to figure it all out."

"Thanks," he said. "I just hope I find the answer before anyone else gets hurt."

15

MONDAY AFTERNOON

When lunch time rolled around, Kristi volunteered to go out for sandwiches for herself and Eula.

The older woman looked up from her piecing and said, "Thanks. I didn't even think about packing a lunch today."

"Any requests?" Kristi asked.

"Well, I was kind of thinking it might be nice to get a sandwich from *The Honey Barrel*." She paused and looked out the window. "You know, support the business in their time of need, what with Herman's death and all."

Kristi shivered. She hadn't told Eula that Herman's partner, Matt Jenkins, had been poisoned last night. She forced a smile and said, "That's a great idea. What would you like?"

"I'm not picky," Eula said, picking up the next square of fabric to piece into the top she was working on, "but maybe something like ham and cheese."

"I bet they'll be able to whip something up," Kristi said, heading to the break room to grab her denim shoulder bag. "I'll be back in a jiffy."

Kristi stepped out of the shop's back door and walked around the side of the small white house that housed *Delectable Mountain*

Quilting. She took a deep breath, inhaling the sweet scents of the flowering bushes she'd planted along the side. The day was sunny and cloudless, a perfect Montana summer day, and she was glad to be outside, if only for a few minutes.

The Honey Barrel Brewpub was located just a few doors down from the quilt shop, but Kristi rarely frequented the place. She thought of it as a glorified bar, though she knew Herman had taken great pride in the deli side of his business. Especially the pickles. Herman had loved pickles and had insisted that the pub keep a large jar of the biggest dill pickles he could find right on the counter where all the customers could see them.

It was ironic that a pickle had killed him.

Shaking her head to clear her thoughts, Kristi pulled open the glass front door of *The Honey Barrel* and stepped inside. A glance at the interior revealed a small restaurant with multiple square four-top tables and a long bar along the back of the room. The floor and walls were rough wood, giving the room a distinctly rustic look. The bar and tables were also dark wood, and the lights, shaped to resemble the type of oil lanterns that she associated with old-time barns, were turned low. She supposed the atmosphere was supposed to be cozy, but with only a few customers scattered among the tables, Kristi found it depressing.

The sole waitress in the room looked up when Kristi stepped inside. Kristi noticed her, too. Young, no more than twenty-five, with medium length blonde hair corralled in two braids that hung over her shoulders, and the kind of peaches and cream complexion and even features that many women longed for.

The attractive young woman stood behind the bar and moved toward the end where the cash register— and huge pickle jar— stood. She started to raise the hinged section, but Kristi waved her back. Walking quickly to the bar at the back of the room, Kristi seated herself on a bar stool and smiled at the young woman.

"No need to come out into the room on my account," she said.

"I'm just looking for a couple of sandwiches to go. Is that a possibility?"

The waitress gave her a wan smile— her eyes were reddened as if she'd been crying. "Of course," she said, handing Kristi a single sheet menu listing lunch items. "What can I get you?"

After perusing the sandwich listings for a moment, Kristi made her decision. "I'll have a *Pulled Porker* and a *Cowboy Club*."

The waitress wrote her choices on an order pad before glancing up. "Anything to drink?"

Kristi waved the suggestion away. "No thanks. We have drinks back at the shop."

The waitress lowered her pad and studied Kristi. "You work around here? I don't think I've seen you before."

Nodding, Kristi held out her hand across the bar. "I'm Kristi Lundrigan. I own the quilt shop down the street... *Delectable Mountain Quilting*."

The young woman shook Kristi's hand. "Vivi Rawlins. I work here." She laughed. "Obviously."

Kristi smiled, then sobered. "I heard about Herman's death." She studied Vivi's face. "I'm so sorry. Eula, my clerk, and I wanted to support a local business through a rough time," she glanced around, "so here I am."

Vivi turned and placed Kristi's order on the shelf to the kitchen. When she turned back, she bit her lower lip before responding. "We appreciate that." She waved around the nearly empty room. "As you can see, we're not exactly overflowing with customers."

Kristi frowned. "Are you usually busy at lunch? I thought maybe your busy time was after work."

Vivi nodded. "It is, but we usually have a steady flow of customers at lunch time, too."

"Maybe folks thought you'd be closed," Kristi suggested.

"Maybe, but Matt..." she paused and took a deep breath. "Matt didn't want to close."

Kristi stretched her hand out to the young woman. "Are you okay?"

She bit her lip again, but after a moment nodded. "It's just, well, Matt was poisoned too. Last night. At Rizzoli's." Her eyes filled with unshed tears. "It just feels like we're being targeted."

Kristi turned her extended hand and rested it on the bar's gleaming surface. "I'm so sorry, Vivi. Is Matt all right? You must be terribly upset."

"It's been hard," Vivi said with a sigh. "First Herman, now Matt... though the doctors say Matt will be fine. I don't know what's going to become of this place."

"Try not to worry," Kristi said, trying to put as much comfort in her voice as she could. "The good news is that Matt will recover, and I'm sure Sheriff Reynolds will find whoever is responsible."

Vivi nodded just as the short order cook rang the little bell and called, "Order's up." She turned, picked the brown paper bag from the shelf and looked inside.

Satisfied, she turned to Kristi. "Here you go. One ham and cheese and one roast beef with bacon and tomato. If you'll step over here, I'll ring that up."

LATER THAT AFTERNOON, Molly Raskin and Elaine Hastings stopped by the shop. When they entered, one right after the other, Eula set her piecing aside and started to get up, but Kristi waved her back down.

"No need to put your project down, Eula," Kristi said. "I've got this." Turning to her customers she asked, "Can I help you with anything?"

Elaine sighed. "Not really. I'm just looking for safe harbor. I figure since you were there, you won't pester me about the poisoned pickles."

Molly nodded. "I'm getting stopped by every other person I meet, too. When I said as much to Elaine, she suggested we come here for a bit."

"I mean, sure, we could just go home," Elaine said with a grimace, "but I'm tired of being cooped up. And it's not as if I did anything wrong!"

"Well, you're both more than welcome here." Kristi grinned. "No purchases necessary."

"Good," Elaine said. "I sure as heck won't be visiting your booth at the fair."

"Definitely not," Molly agreed. "I'm not sure I'll ever set foot on the fairgrounds again!"

Kristi studied the woman. She knew Elaine well, but Molly was only an occasional customer. She judged Molly to be in her mid-thirties, a petite woman with dark, wavy, shoulder length hair. She had an upturned nose, a rounded chin, and plump, pink cheeks.

"Not to prod a sore subject, but did you have pickles entered, Molly?"

The woman's eyes widened. "Yes! And it's been just awful. First a deputy questioned me, and then the sheriff came to my house and asked if he could see my canning supplies!" She paused and took a dramatic breath. "Can you imagine? The sheriff! In my house... looking through my things!" She shook her head. "It was just *awful*! It was like he thought I'd killed..."

She stopped abruptly and lowered her eyes. "I'm sorry, Elaine," she said quietly. "I forgot. He actually arrested you."

Elaine waved the comment away. "Not technically, but I did have to go to the sheriff's office with him and answer a lot of questions." She smiled at Kristi. "Fortunately, Kristi was there to hold my hand, and Jason was actually really nice to me."

"Jason?" Molly's eyes got even wider, something Kristi wouldn't have thought possible.

Elaine nodded. "Sheriff Reynolds. His first name is Jason."

"You know his first name?"

"Well, he and Kristi…"

"Jason and I are dating," Kristi said quickly. "And since Elaine and I are friends, she's met him several times… without being arrested."

Molly eyed Kristi speculatively, but giggled. "I had no idea."

"So," Kristi said, hoping to change the subject, "any thoughts on who the culprit might be?"

"I haven't got a clue," Elaine said, with a sad little frown, "but I hear the deputies have moved on from those of us who had pickles entered to the volunteers who were working the judging."

"Oh! That can't be right," Molly said, shaking her head. "Rhonda Gervais won the division so often that she stopped entering and started volunteering."

"And Jaci Evans," Elaine added, "is just a girl. She's still in high school."

"And she's Rhonda's granddaughter," Molly said. "I can't imagine either one of them poisoning pickles!"

"Wasn't there one other woman helping out that day?" Kristi asked.

Molly and Elaine looked at each other, both frowning in concentration. Finally Elaine snapped her fingers, her eyebrows lifting. "Yes! Delilah Robinson. But she never enters the canning division."

"That's right," agreed Molly. "Delilah is a baker. As far as I know, she doesn't make pickles."

"Well," said Kristi. "I'm sure Jason will find the guilty party. For now, enough about pickles and murder. Let's talk quilting!"

By the time Molly and Elaine left, each with several yards of quilting cottons, they both looked much more relaxed than they'd been when they arrived. The shop's gorgeous fabrics and endless pattern possibilities had worked their magic once again.

MONDAY EVENING

After closing the shop and taking the day's receipts to the bank, Kristi drove home. When she unlocked the kitchen door and stepped inside, both cats rushed to greet her.

"What's this?" she asked as Stitches pranced back and forth in front of her and Between wound around her legs. "It's not like I've been gone for a week!"

Stepping carefully around the excited felines, she quickly checked the rest of the house. Nothing was missing, and nothing appeared to have been disturbed. The front door was still securely locked. No burglars hid in any of the closets.

All was well in the house. So what had the cats so excited?

She discovered the probable cause when she opened the front door to peer outside. A large vase of flowers, carnations and baby's breath to be exact, rested on the porch. When she brought them inside, she found a note from Jason.

"Oh," she said to the cats, "I see. Jason was here, but he didn't come in and give you the attention you deserve." She nodded. "I'd be upset too. But all is well, I'm here, and I'll pet you."

She placed the vase of flowers on the coffee table, plucked the note from among the blooms, and sat down to read it while petting first one cat, then the other.

Kristi, sorry I can't join you at Mark and Stacy's tonight. Please give them my regrets and have fun. I'll try to see you at the fair tomorrow. Love, Jason.

She sighed. Well, that was too bad. She'd been looking forward to having dinner with Jason at Mark and Stacy's.

After a few final chin scritches for each kitty-kid, Kristi headed to her bedroom to freshen up for her dinner date.

A short while later she pulled her red Subaru Outback into the driveway behind Stacy's forest green Ford Taurus. Smiling to herself, she thought about how the purchase of *Delectable Mountain Quilting* had led to her friendship with both Stacy and her new husband, Mark. Stacy had been her real estate agent, and Kristi had hired Mark to renovate the shop before she opened her business. They'd each become a friend before they found each other and started dating.

Kristi wished she could take credit for introducing them, but they'd come together with no help from her whatsoever.

Well... she had made the Christmas Star quilt that had played a part in Mark's proposal, but he was a determined man. He'd have proposed even without the quilt.

Laughing at herself, Kristi stepped out of her car and walked up to the couple's front porch. Mark had remodeled the home's interior, but the exterior, at least the curb-facing part, was original— a pale blue 1950s three-bedroom bungalow, single-storied with a sloping roof and wide, covered front porch. Mark's renovation had included a new master bedroom suite, so the house now boasted four bedrooms.

Stacy opened the front door before Kristi even had a chance to knock.

"You're here!" Stacy gave her a one-armed squeeze and ushered her inside. "I was afraid you'd cancel when Jason couldn't come."

Kristi shook her head. "If I had to cancel every invitation Jason couldn't make, I'd never see anyone. The sheriff's department keeps him entirely too busy."

Mark stepped into the living room and greeted Kristi. "I bet he's especially busy right now, what with the poisoning at the fair."

"Not to mention last night's second act," Kristi said somberly.

Stacy stared at her. "What do you mean?"

"Oh," Kristi said, covering her mouth and collapsing into an overstuffed chair. "I probably shouldn't have said that."

"Well, you did," Mark pointed out, pulling Stacy to the couch. When both were seated, he said, "Out with it. Don't leave us hanging. What happened?"

"You know, of course, that Herman Studebakker died, right?"

"Yes," Mark said, "and that Mama Rizzoli and Silvi Kuhlman were hospitalized."

"Okay. So last night, Herman's business partner, Matt Jenkins, was also poisoned. At *Rizzoli's Fine Italian Restaurant*."

"Oh, wow," Stacy said, faintly. "He didn't die, did he?"

"Not as far as I know. Jason said he was rushed to the hospital though."

"Same type of poison?" Mark asked.

Kristi shrugged. "Last I heard Jason was still waiting for that to be determined by the lab."

Stacy stood and gestured toward the dining room. "And on that pleasant note, let's eat."

Mark laughed, but Kristi cringed.

"Sorry, Stace," she said. "I didn't mean to put a damper on dinner."

Before Stacy could respond, Mark said, "No worries. Stace knows *nothing* dims my appetite... except of course her excellent cooking."

Stacy swatted his arm, but looked much happier.

After a wonderful dinner of roast beef, red potatoes, asparagus, and mixed fruit, they moved back to the living room for coffee and chocolate cake.

When everyone was seated with their dessert, Mark said, "I heard you were there when the poisoning happened at the fair. Is that true?"

Kristi nodded. "My friend, Elaine Hastings, had pickles entered in that division. Mattie and I were there to support her."

"Oh, poor Elaine," Stacy said. "That must have been traumatic for her."

"It was." Kristi glanced at her chocolate cake, trying to decide how much to say.

"Nobody suspected Elaine, did they?" Stacy asked.

Kristi glanced up, met Stacy's gaze, and nodded. "For a while, everyone thought the jar of pickles was Elaine's. Her *dill delights* were the next pickles that were scheduled to be judged."

Stacy's hand flew to her mouth. She and Elaine had a certain history. Elaine had been Mattie's best friend since childhood, and prior to his death, Stacy had been having an affair with Mattie's husband. Mattie and Stacy, while they'd never be good friends, had made peace with each other. But Elaine... well Kristi understood that it was hard to forgive someone who had hurt a dear friend. Still, neither woman wished the other ill.

Mark, who knew the whole story, scooted closer to his wife and put his arm around her.

"But," Stacy said quietly, "you said *for a while*, Elaine's not still a suspect is she?"

Kristi shook her head. "No. Jason found evidence that cleared her."

Stacy's eyes slid shut. "Thank heavens."

"Does Jason have any viable suspects?" Mark asked.

Kristi gave a wry laugh. "That's the problem. He has too many suspects. Lots of people with opportunity— the volunteers, the spectators, the pickle makers, people just walking past the judges' area— but he hasn't found a real motive." She set her coffee and cake on the coffee table and shook her head. "I mean, he doesn't even know for sure who the target was. I tend to focus on Herman because he died, but that was because of a drug interaction. It's possible that Mama or Silvi was the target and the poisoner simply didn't know that Herman was taking a really strong heart medication."

Mark nodded. "I'm guessing the fact that Matt was poisoned at *Rizzoli's* doesn't really shed any light."

Kristi sighed. "Too true. Does it mean someone has it out for *Rizzoli's* and Mama was the original target, or is someone trying to wipe out *The Honey Barrel*?"

"Wow, it sounds like a really complex puzzle," Stacy said.

Mark looked thoughtful. "Of course, if it turns out Matt was simply suffering from a stomach bug, things will look different."

"That's true too." Picking up her coffee cup, Kristi took a sip before continuing. "But enough of this depressing subject. What have you two been up to?"

The rest of the evening passed in light-hearted conversation. So much so, that by the time she headed home to her kitty-kids, Kristi felt calm and refreshed. A night out with friends was just what she'd needed.

17

TUESDAY MORNING

Kristi's feelings of contentment didn't extend to the next morning. She woke feeling less than rested. Her sleep had been disturbed by dark dreams. Nothing bad enough to qualify as actual nightmares, and nothing note worthy enough to be remembered in the light of day. Just depressing, and disquieting enough that she'd roused multiple times during the night.

Nothing horrific, but bad enough that when morning finally arrived she didn't feel rested. And she certainly wasn't in a bright, cheerful mood as she went through the motions of getting ready to go to work at the fairgrounds.

"I'm sorry I ever thought about setting up a booth at the fair," she said, looking at Stitches' reflection in the bathroom mirror and pointing her hairbrush at the tabby. "If I didn't have a booth, I wouldn't have been at the pickle judging, and I wouldn't have seen a man murdered."

Stitches stared at her a moment longer, then dropped to her side and began grooming her fur.

Kristi snorted. "You're right. That wouldn't have changed anything. I'd still have gone to the judging to support Elaine." She finished brushing her long, blonde hair and put the brush away.

Dividing her heavy hair into three sections, she pulled it over her shoulder and wove the sections into a thick braid. "Maybe the problem is friends. If I didn't have any friends, I wouldn't be worried about them."

The ludicrousness of that statement made her laugh out loud. Of course she cared about her friends. What kind of person would she be if she didn't? She finished the braid, grabbed a coated elastic band, and wrapped it around the end to hold them together.

Stitches, recognizing the end of Kristi's morning hair routine, stood, stretched and stepped out of the bathroom into the bedroom with Kristi close behind. Between jumped off the bed and joined Stitches in leading Kristi to the kitchen where breakfast would be served. The little black tuxedo cat pranced happily into the hall, his tail high.

Kristi smiled. Stitches and Between knew her routine as well as she did. Their very presence lightened her mood and banished the last wisps of her unsatisfactory night from her mind.

"All right, kitty-kids," she said. "You're right. Time for breakfast." She followed the cats into the kitchen. "What will it be this morning? Egg and kibble, or kibble and egg?"

The cats took up their usual waiting-for-breakfast positions and stared at her, as if to say "quit being silly and feed us."

"Egg and kibble it is." Kristi opened the refrigerator and pulled out the covered covered dish holding the sliced hard-boiled egg she'd saved for the cats. After evaluating the number of slices left, she shrugged and placed the container on the floor in front of the cats with a flourish.

"Your egg is served, your majesties."

While the cats shared the hard-boiled egg slices, she shook kibble into their food bowl, before turning back to the refrigerator.

"Decisions, decisions. What should I have for breakfast?"

After considering her options, she poured herself a glass of orange juice, fixed a bowl of her favorite multi-grain cereal, splashed on some milk, and carried her breakfast to the breakfast table with its view of the Absaroka Mountains.

The view calmed her, as it always did. Clear blue skies that seemed to stretch forever, until they bunched up against the mountain grandeur. The occasional white cloud sailing serenely over the valley, pulling its shadow across the wide pasture land. The grassland dotted with cattle, the fence lines barely discernible at this distance. The foothills stepping into tall, craggy mountains, their slopes gradually changing from the dark green of pine forests to the steely blue-gray of granite peaks and precipices.

As she scooped up the last bite of cereal, Kristi thought again how lucky she was to have found this house, with this fabulous view. Not to mention how lucky she was to live in Montana. She couldn't imagine living anywhere else. The winters might be extreme, but the summers were magnificent.

She sighed and tore her gaze away from the view. The summer day might be amazing, but she had responsibilities. Right now, she needed to get a move on. Time to head to the fair.

A half-hour later, Kristi parked her red Subaru Outback in the exhibitor's lot and, enjoying the early morning sunshine, headed to the booth. She was scheduled to work with Mattie today while Ruby and Andrea held down the fort at the shop. She was glad Eula had the day off. If the older woman had been here at the fair, it would have felt too similar to Saturday... and Kristi really didn't want to think about Saturday.

Showing her exhibitor badge to the security officer at the door, Kristi stepped into the building's cool interior. If felt dim after the bright sunshine outdoors, but she knew her eyes would adjust momentarily.

"Hey, Kristi," a familiar voice said from behind her. She squinted over her shoulder and found Mattie just stepping inside after showing off her own badge.

"Morning, Mattie," Kristi said, smiling at her friend and employee. "Ready to demonstrate hand quilting this morning?"

Mattie grinned and held up a pretty, pieced and quilted bag. "I sure am. Brought a project I've been working on at home."

The two continued chatting once they reached their booth and set about getting ready for the day. When the doors of the exhibition hall opened, the two women were more than ready to greet potential customers as well as fair-goers who were merely curious about quilting.

The morning was nicely busy. The booth was never over-crowded, but the stream of customers and browsers was constant. Mattie cut several orders while Kristi rang up the sales and dealt with the payments. By the time Mattie settled into her chair to do her hand quilting demonstration, Kristi was ready for a break. She leaned against the cutting table and watched as several women clustered around Mattie.

Pulling the pretty bag from beneath a table, Mattie pulled a small lap quilt from inside.

"This is a project I've been working on at home," she explained, "so the hoop is already in place." She indicated the wooden quilting hoop as she settled the quilt in her lap. "You'll notice the hoop looks a lot like an embroidery hoop, only much larger and sturdier."

Next she talked her audience through the difference between a regular needle and the tiny, sharp quilting between as well as the importance of using quilting thread and how to choose an appropriate thimble.

When all was in readiness, Mattie demonstrated, explaining as she did so, how to load the short needle with several stitches and, using the thimble she wore on her middle finger, push the needle through the layers.

"And that's how you hand quilt," she said as she loaded the needle once again. "But you do need to be careful, especially while you're learning. Try not to stab the needle down. You don't want to prick the finger that's underneath," she said. "Blood on the backing is not at all attractive."

The ladies laughed, but one asked a question. "Why don't you wear a thimble on the finger that's under the quilt?"

Mattie kept her needle moving, but glanced at the questioner. "That's an excellent question," she said, "and one I asked my grandmother when she was teaching me how to do this. I didn't like the idea of stabbing myself anymore than you do."

The woman smiled.

"The reason I don't protect my index finger is simple: I need to be able to feel the needle as it comes through the layers of fabric. A thimble protects my finger, but it also keeps me from being aware of the needle." Mattie smiled. "Trust me, once you get accustomed to the action, you won't stab yourself. You'll figure out just how much pressure you need to apply and you'll learn to rock the needle as soon as you feel it come through."

She rested the hoop in her lap and pulled both hands into view. "See? No bloody fingers!"

Mattie continued quilting and answering questions until her observers began drifting away. When the last woman left, she folded the lap quilt around her hoop and stowed it back in her bag.

"That went well," Kristi said when Mattie joined her at the cutting table.

"Thanks. It was fun."

"A few of the ladies asked me if you taught hand quilting at the shop," Kristi said as she reshelved a bolt of pink floral fabric. "Would you be interested in teaching a class?"

Mattie picked up a bolt of sea green batik and returned it to its shelf while she considered the question.

"I could be," she finally said, "though you'd want to check with Ruby too. She's also a hand quilter."

Kristi nodded. "I'm aware. I've observed her demos as well, but no one asked me about classes after hers." Kristi paused to pick up another bolt of fabric before continuing. "I'm a machine quilter through and through, so when I set up the class schedule, I didn't even think about a hand quilting class. But if there's interest, and if you or Ruby would be willing to teach, we could certainly add one to the schedule."

"I doubt you'd get many to sign up," Mattie said with a sigh. "Most people who are just getting started prefer faster results."

"Yes, but hand quilting is an art form, and it shouldn't be lost. So even though I don't do it, we should still try to keep it alive."

"True," Mattie agreed. A little crease appeared between her eyes and she cocked her head as she glanced at Kristi. "Didn't you tell me your grandmother taught you to quilt? How did you escape hand quilting?"

Kristi laughed. "Yes, Nanna Van Oss infected me with the quilting bug… but she failed to get me to hand quilt. She tried, but I wasn't interested, and I was a terrible student. I never managed to catch the rhythm, plus I was constantly stabbing myself. As soon as I discovered the rotary cutter and mat, I was much more at home designing quilts and piecing and quilting them on a sewing machine. Nanna gave in, deciding that as long as I was quilting, the tools I chose were inconsequential."

Mattie grinned. "A wise woman!"

"Indeed." Kristi studied the fabrics surrounding her and gave a curt nod. "The tools may be inconsequential, but we should offer all of them to our customers. I'll check with Ruby, but let me know your availability and we'll get a hand quilting class scheduled."

Mattie nodded. "That sounds great."

18

TUESDAY AFTERNOON

With no additional demos scheduled, the customer flow tapered off to just a few curious browsers. Just before noon, Kristi handed Mattie the company credit card and sent her off to buy lunch at the food court.

Kristi answered a few questions from browsers, but the booth was empty when Mattie returned with their food. They turned a corner of the cutting table into a lunch counter and pulled up chairs. Mattie unpacked the food. A State Fair Sub for each of them and a serving of nachos to share.

After grabbing a couple of bottles of water from the cooler under a table, they settled down to eat. Kristi's first bite of her sub caused her to close her eyes in bliss. Juicy Italian sausage smothered in cheese and onions, all layered on crispy French bread. What was there not to love? And combined with tortilla chips drenched in even more cheese, well, Mattie had found the perfect meal.

Swallowing the flavorful bite, Kristi murmured, "There's nothing like fair food!"

Mattie laughed. "That sounded reminiscent of *There's no place like home.*

Opening her eyes, Kristi nodded. "They're similar, very similar."

Grabbing a chip loaded with cheese, Mattie asked, "So... who do you think poisoned the judges?"

Kristi sipped some water before responding. "Honestly? I have absolutely no clue." She picked up her sub, but hesitated to take a bite until after asking, "What about you? Any suspicions?"

Mattie paused before popping another cheesy chip into her mouth. "Not really, but I'm guessing at least one of the volunteers was involved."

Kristi nodded, chewed, and swallowed. "It does seem unlikely that someone not involved in the judging would be able to get that jar of tainted pickles into the line-up." She drank some more water. "Do you know the volunteers?"

Mattie shook her head. "By name only. I think Elaine said there were three on duty, Rhonda Gervais, Delilah Robinson, and Jaci Evans."

"But Jaci is just a teen, isn't she?

"Yep. She's also Rhonda's granddaughter. Elaine said Rhonda used to win most of the canning categories, but stopped competing a few years back. I think she's trying to tempt Jaci into following in her footsteps."

"Got it," Kristi said. "Kind of like our grandmothers pulled us into quilting."

Mattie toasted Kristi with her water bottle. "Exactly. Passing on the skill you love."

"What about Delilah?"

"Again, here-say from Elaine. Delilah still enters the food divisions, but never canning. She's a master baker."

They ate in silence for a few moments while Kristi considered the volunteers. Finally she sighed and shook her head.

"I just can't see any reason any of those women would want to poison one, or all, of the judges. Have you heard of any bad feelings between any of them."

Mattie shook her head. "Nothing that I've ever heard."

"What about another pickle maker? Any thoughts there?"

"Well," Mattie said after taking a moment to finish the final bite of her sub, "the only ones I know besides Elaine are customers of ours. I sure hope none of them was involved."

Kristi agreed. "Who?"

"Molly Raskin."

"Right. She and Elaine stopped by the shop yesterday. Said they weren't really comfortable at the fairgrounds at the moment. Who else?"

"Mavis Johnson."

"Isn't she the reigning 'pickle queen'?" Kristi asked. At Mattie's nod, she shook her head. "I can't see Mavis disrupting the judging. Not if she hoped to continue her winning streak."

Mattie shrugged. "Maybe she was worried about Elaine taking her crown. Those were supposed to be Elaine's pickles that were being judged when they all got sick."

"That's true." Kristi used the final chip to scoop up the remaining creamy cheese sauce. "Herman probably wasn't supposed to die, so it could've been an attempt to discredit Elaine." She popped the chip in her mouth and chewed thoughtfully. "Still, Mavis has been up against other pickle makers for years. Poisoning seems extreme for a blue ribbon. Do you know anything about her?"

Mattie didn't answer immediately. Instead she picked up their trash and tossed it in a nearby garbage container. Once she was seated again, she met Kristi's gaze straight on.

"Mavis and my mother were best friends. They've known each other since they were girls, so I've known Mavis my whole life." She took a deep breath and let it out slowly. "A few years ago I would've said she wasn't capable of such a thing, but..."

"But a few years ago you would've said your mother wasn't capable of murder," Kristi finished for her friend. "Mattie, I'm so sorry."

Before Kristi could say anything else, a group of women entered the booth, chatting among themselves and directing the occasional question to Kristi or Mattie.

Poisoned pickles took a back seat to discussions of the Pickle Dish quilt block and Kristi's upcoming class.

The remainder of the afternoon passed in a busy blur of cutting and folding, reshelving, and the ever-so-satisfying recording of sales in the app on their tablet. Before she knew it, Kristi and Mattie were closing the booth down for the night and walking to their cars.

"It was a good day," Kristi said when she reached her Subaru. "Thanks for all your hard work, Mattie."

Waving away Kristi's words, Mattie said, "Whether you own it or I own it, I love that shop. You've done a good job juggling the shop and the booth. I wouldn't have tackled it." She laughed. "Actually, I never did try for a booth at the fair in all the years I owned *Delectable Mountain Quilting*. Selling to you was the best thing I ever did for the shop!"

Kristi grinned. "I'm glad you think so! Have a good day at the shop tomorrow."

"I will," Mattie said. "I'm looking forward to the familiarity of the shop after a day at the fair."

With that they parted company, each to their own car and a solitary drive home.

TUESDAY EVENING

Jason's white Trail Blazer pulled into Kristi's driveway just after she did. They nodded to each other, each carrying a small grocery bag, and entered the house together through the kitchen door.

If the cats were surprised by Jason's appearance, they kept it to themselves, reacting to his presence with supreme indifference. At least until Kristi and Jason set their bags on the kitchen counter. Then the possibility of food set Stitches to winding between Kristi's legs. After a moment's hesitation, Between performed the same service for Jason.

Kristi smiled at Jason as she pulled containers out of her bag. "The kitty-kids are glad you're here."

He glanced at the little black tuxedo cat winding around his legs and said, "As long as he doesn't trip me when I'm walking."

"He won't," she assured him. "They're very careful when I'm moving."

He nodded. "He probably doesn't want to be stepped on any more than I want to be tripped."

Jason had called before Kristi had even managed to exit the fairgrounds parking lot, suggesting they have dinner together.

Since neither of them was really interested in sitting in a restaurant where people could pester Jason for information, they'd decided on take-out. Kristi would bring the main course, while Jason handled drinks and dessert.

"Hope you like fried chicken," she said.

He glanced at her. "Doesn't everyone?"

She laughed.

"Where should I put this?" he asked, holding up a pint of pralines and cream ice cream.

She nodded toward the refrigerator. "Should be space in the freezer. Good choice, by the way."

He put the ice cream in the freezer section before opening the refrigerator and stowing a six-pack of her favorite cola.

She'd finished unpacking the food containers and was pulling out plates, utensils, and serving spoons. When all was in readiness, they heaped their plates with fried chicken, coleslaw, potato salad, and soft rolls.

Together, they headed to the table, glancing first at the breakfast table, then at the dining room. As if thinking the same thing, they glanced at each other, grinned, and strode to the living room instead. Kristi plopped on one end of the couch, her plate and napkin in her lap, ice-cold cola on a coaster on the end table at her side, and Jason settled in a similar position at the other end.

"This looks great," he said, and gesturing to the couch added, "and about as far from formal dining as we could get."

"Agreed. This is all about comfort. After all," she said after a sip of cola, "it's been a long day. Comfort is called for."

Jason nodded, but contented himself with biting into his crunchy fried chicken. When their meals had been consumed, they placed their plates on the coffee table, wiped greasy fingers on cloth napkins, and sat back with contented sighs.

"How was…" they said simultaneously.

Kristi laughed and toasted Jason with the remains of her cola. "You first."

He grinned. "I was just going to ask how your day was?"

"It was good. Mattie did a very successful hand quilting demo. So successful that I had people asking if we teach it at the shop. I talked to Mattie about it and we're going to add a class to the schedule. Next week. After we recover from the fair." She paused for a sip of cola before asking, "How was your day? Any new leads on the poisoner?"

He shook his head. "It's slow going. We've interviewed everyone we can think of and so far have come up empty on the motive. Lots of opportunity. Plenty of means. But the motive is missing, and until I understand that, it'll be hard to solve this one."

Kristi curled her legs into a more comfortable position and pointed sternly to each of the cats. They were slinking in what they obviously considered a stealthy manner toward the plates on the coffee table. When they realized Kristi was watching, Between flopped onto his side and Stitches shot a leg in the air and started grooming.

"What about Matt Jenkins? Was he poisoned with hemlock, too?"

"Yep. The lab got back to me yesterday afternoon about that. Same type of hemlock, too."

"There are different types?"

He nodded. "There's a tree— not poisonous; and the weed— a deadly poison. And then there's commercially created hemlock which is used in several medicinal products. All of our poisonings have been from the weed. Even Matt Jenkins."

"So no viable suspects yet?"

"Not yet."

"Mattie and I were discussing possible perps."

"Perps?" His voice held just a hint of a smile.

"You know, perpetrators."

He grinned and shook his head. "You've been watching too much TV."

Her cheeks heated and she narrowed her eyes. "Well, what would you call them?"

"Suspects."

"Fine," she said with a huff. "We were discussing possible *suspects.*"

"Did you come up with any answers."

"Of course not! We're not detectives."

His expression sobered. "Just as long as you remember that, Kristi. I don't want you getting hurt again." He waited a moment, then asked, "What did you come up with?"

"We were mainly thinking of the volunteers— Jaci's too young, and Rhonda and Delilah don't have any reason to hurt anyone— and pickle makers, but we only know two besides Elaine."

"Who?"

"Molly Raskin and Mavis Johnson. Both are quilters and customers... and really nice ladies." She bit her lip.

"But..." he urged her to continue.

"But Mavis is a close friend of Velma Carson's."

"Ah," he said. "Guilt by association."

She nodded. "I know. Totally unfair to even think it, but..."

"But you did."

She lowered her eyes and fiddled with the hem of her shirt.

"Personally, I think if Mavis was looking for revenge for Velma, she'd poison one of us," he said quietly. "Not the pickle judges at the fair."

Kristi blew out a breath. "You're absolutely right. So, not only did we not solve anything, we thought unkind things about a customer... and someone Mattie has known all her life. We suck."

Jason slid across the couch and put his arms around her. "Don't worry. I'm not going to tell anyone." He kissed her forehead. "Besides, investigating people you know is tricky. You have to be careful of preconceived ideas."

He tilted her head back and kissed her on the mouth, gently at first, then with more passion. Their tongues danced and the heat built until she was clinging to him.

When he finally lifted his head, he studied her for a moment. "You're very precious to me, Kristi. Promise me you won't try to investigate the poisonings. Promise me you'll let me and my deputies handle it."

She gazed into his eyes and saw nothing but love and concern. "You drive a hard bargain, Sheriff," she said in a breathy voice, "but I promise."

He pulled her against his chest and held her tightly before lifting her chin and kissing her again. Very thoroughly.

Her heart raced and her insides liquified. This. She'd missed this so much. Running her fingers through his wavy chestnut hair; the rasp of his unshaven chin against her cheek; the feel of his heavily muscled chest against her body.

Divorced or not, this was her man. Her one and only love. Her destiny. She would love Jason until she died, and being in his arms again was the only heaven she could imagine.

She wanted him. She always would.

His lips skimmed her neck, her cheek. He nibbled her earlobe. "I want to spend the night," he whispered. "Let me love you, Kristi!"

"Yes," she said, her word little more than a breath. "Take me to bed, Jason." She pulled away from him, though it wrenched her to do so, and met his hot gaze directly. "Now."

He stood, scooped her into his arms, and strode to the bedroom. "I'm at your command." He paused in the doorway to kiss her again. "Always."

20

WEDNESDAY MORNING

Kristi stretched awake, her foot sliding against a decidedly masculine shin. She didn't open her eyes, but smiled into her pillow. She hadn't dreamed the earth-shaking delights of the previous night after all. Jason was here. In her bed. The world had righted itself; they were back together, as they always should have been.

Opening her eyes, she peeked at him through her lashes. Long and lean, his powerful body covered with nothing but a sheet, he lay sprawled on his stomach, still soundly sleeping. She should probably still be asleep as well. They'd had a *very* active night, making love more times than they'd ever managed in a single night as a married couple.

Almost as though they were trying to make up for all the time they'd spent apart. All in the space of single night.

She stretched again, luxuriating in the bliss of a well-loved body. She couldn't remember the last time she'd felt so content, so at peace. Why she could almost purr!

Purr! Her eyes flew open and she raised her head to scan the room. Where were the cats? They were always on the bed when she woke up. Mind you, her bed had never been so *active* before this. Stitches and Between had never before experienced a man spending the night.

She was about to get up when Jason stirred, flinging his arm across her and pulling her toward him as if she were his personal teddy bear. She grinned and snuggled closer. She could get used to being cuddled first thing in the morning by a still sleeping man. At least, she could if that man was Jason!

Jason. The man she loved. The only man she'd ever loved... or ever would.

She traced her finger along his jaw enjoying the sandpaper feel of his stubble, pushed a wayward lock of his wavy chestnut hair from his face, then leaned in and kissed those fabulously soft lips. She'd forgotten how soft his lips could be.

He responded by pulling her closer, his eyes opening slowly. A smile spread across those fabulous lips. "Good morning," he said, his voice nearly as raspy as his unshaven chin. "Last night was real, wasn't it. Not just another dream after all."

She laughed quietly. "Have you dreamed of me often?"

His eyes widened. "Every damn night," he said. "And been disappointed every morning." His smile widened. "Except today. This morning you're here, which means last night really happened."

"Oh, it happened, Sheriff," she said punctuating her words with kisses along his jaw and neck, "over and over and over again."

He growled. "I think we need another performance, just to make sure we covered all the bases!"

He turned her onto her back and was moving on top of her when his cell phone rang. Frowning, he glanced at the bedside table where he'd left it and noticed the clock. Leaning over, he grabbed the phone, but before he answered, he let out a string of swear words, ending with, "Is that the time?"

"Sure is," Kristi said, sliding out from under him and heading to the bathroom. "You'd better answer that," she called over her shoulder. "I hear you're the sheriff. Might be important."

She heard him say, "Sheriff Reynolds," as she closed the bathroom door, giving him privacy for his official role.

When she returned to the bedroom, Jason was up and dressing and both cats sprawled on the tangled mess of bedsheets. Nodding, she finished tying the belt of her terry bathrobe. That hadn't taken long. The cats were adjusting to Jason's presence just fine.

"Well," Jason said, striding to her side, "this isn't how I'd planned to spend the next half-hour or so, but duty calls." He kissed her lightly, then frowned as he touched his chin. "You don't happen to have a razor do you?"

"Only the one I use on my legs," she answered with a grin, "and I wouldn't recommend it."

He shook his head as he stepped into the bathroom. "No shave for me this morning then."

Kristi padded out into the kitchen, followed closely by the cats. After giving them their morning kibble, she studied the refrigerator wondering if she had time to scramble some eggs before he had to leave.

"Don't worry about breakfast," he called as he came toward her from the bedroom. "No time this morning. They've got a bit of an emergency down at the department." He stopped beside her and kissed her lightly. "Let's make a habit of this, okay?"

"Fine by me," she answered. "See you tonight?"

He grabbed his Stetson from the hook beside her purse and keys where he'd left it the night before, his other hand on the door, but looked back at her over his shoulder. His steely gray eyes had gone blue with emotion, and she shivered when she saw them. "Is that an invitation?"

She nodded. "Absolutely. A standing one."

His grip on the doorknob tightened, and she could almost feel him fighting the desire to turn around and take her back to bed.

But duty won. He simply nodded, opened the door, and walked out.

Kristi released the breath she hadn't realized she'd been holding, hugged herself, and bounced on her toes. "He wanted to stay," she called to the cats as she twirled around the kitchen. "He wanted to stay and make love to me again." She stopped and steadied herself against the counter. "But he's a good man. A responsible man. So he left to be the sheriff instead." Putting her fingers on her lips, she smiled remembering all the kisses they'd shared. "And I love him even more for it!"

It took her longer than usual, but Kristi finally managed to come down from her cloud of happiness long enough to get dressed and drive to the fairgrounds. Everything seemed brighter this morning. The day was gorgeous, clear blue sky, a few white puffy clouds, warm sunshine highlighting the town with a golden glow. Why even the gravel and dirt parking lot at the fairgrounds seemed to shine. She was so ebullient she practically floated to the booth where Ruby was busy getting things ready for the day.

"Good morning, Ruby," she practically sang.

Ruby stopped rearranging fat quarters and turned to stare at her. "Good morning to you too," she said, studying Kristi quizzically. "You're in an unusually good mood this morning."

Kristi grinned and nodded. "It's a gorgeous day and we're at the fair. Who doesn't love a fair?"

"Hmmm." Ruby bit her lip, nodded and said, "Let's just go with that. It's going to be a great day at the fair!"

21

WEDNESDAY AFTERNOON

It actually did turn out to be a great day at the fair. At least at the *Delectable Mountain Quilting* booth. Kristi did her demo on how to machine piece the Pickle Dish block mid-morning. Her audience was enthusiastic, and several women signed up for next month's class.

Mavis Johnson, the reigning pickle queen and one of the shop's many customers, stopped by to observe the demo, and Kristi had to admit that she seemed like a perfectly nice older woman. She definitely didn't give off a vibe that said, *Cross me and I'll poison your pickles,* even if she had been a close friend of Velma Carson's.

Kristi tried really hard not to think about Velma. The woman might be Mattie's mother, but she was clearly deranged. Not only had she shot Mattie's husband Gary dead— over a *quilt* for pity's sake!— she'd also threatened Kristi's life. Actually, Velma shot Kristi too, but thanks to Jason's intervention, Kristi had lived.

Jason. Now there was someone worth thinking about!

The sheriff had stopped by the booth at lunchtime and Kristi had taken a quick break to stroll over to the food court with him. Ostensibly to buy lunch for herself and Ruby, but Ruby had seen right through that ruse and had given the two of them a knowing smile before they left the booth.

Now, sitting at the corner of the cutting table with Ruby eating a corn dog and sharing a tray of nachos during a brief lull in booth traffic, Kristi felt like she'd been sleepwalking through the last two years. After last night, everything seemed to have come into focus. Colors were brighter. People were more interesting. Life was just… glorious!

"So," Ruby said, swiping a tortilla chip through the creamy cheese sauce, "you and the sheriff?"

Kristi tried to maintain a nonchalant attitude, but couldn't keep a small smile from curling the corners of her mouth. "What about us?"

"I knew you were dating," Ruby said, "but something seems different today."

"Really?" Kristi said, trying to make her voice as innocent sounding as she could. "I can't imagine what."

Ruby laughed. "I can," she murmured, then said in a conversational tone, "but it's none of my business, so… what time do you want me to do my demo?"

Kristi grinned, gratefully accepting the change of subject. "I can't remember, have we advertised a time?"

Ruby shook her head. "We did on my first one, but with everything that's happened we've kind of let that detail slip."

"No problem," Kristi said with a nod. "Just pick a time when we have people in the booth and go for it."

"Sounds good."

"I bet once you start, more people will stop to watch," Kristi said. "Oh! I almost forgot. Mattie and I were talking about scheduling a hand quilting class. Would you be interested in teaching? Either on your own, or with Mattie?"

Ruby's eyes sparkled, making her whole face light up. "Would I! I'd love to, though if we have very many people sign up, we might be better off team teaching. Hand quilting takes a bit of individualized attention while you're learning."

Kristi nodded. "I agree. Even with Nanna watching my every move, I never did get the hang of it." She smiled. "No loss there. I love machine piecing and quilting."

Several women wandered into the booth. Kristi greeted them while Ruby whisked the remains of their lunch into a trash bin. Break time was over.

An hour or so later, Ruby pulled out her hand quilting supplies and started her demonstration. She'd barely begun when a teenage girl and a woman Kristi assumed was her mother stepped into the booth.

Kristi frowned. The teen looked familiar, but Kristi was certain the older woman wasn't a customer. She was sure she'd never seen the girl either here in the booth or at the shop. Where had she come across this particular teen?

When the memory surfaced, Kristi took an involuntary step back. That was Jaci Evans, one of the volunteers at the pickle judging. She was sure of it. Wondering what the girl was doing in her booth, Kristi approached the two.

"Welcome to *Delectable Mountain Quilting*," she said. "I'm Kristi Lundrigan, the owner. Can I help you find anything?"

The mother figure answered, "I don't think so. We're just looking, aren't we Jaci."

Bingo! "Oh," Kristi said. "You're Jaci Evans, aren't you? I saw you at the pickle judging. My friend, Elaine Hastings, had dill pickles entered." She turned to the mother figure. "Are you Jaci's mother? You must've been so worried when all those judges got sick."

The woman's face blanched, but she answered calmly. "Yes. I'm Allyson Evans. My daughter and mother were both there." Her gaze turned cold. "We were all traumatized. We'd prefer not to talk about it."

Kristi glanced at Jaci. The girl looked terrified. Much more so than talking about something that had happened several days ago seemed to warrant. Kristi was about to comment on Jaci's expression when Allyson grabbed her daughter's arm and steered her out of the booth and away from Kristi. Just before the crowded aisle swallowed them, Allyson threw a nasty glance at Kristi.

Interesting. Why was Jaci still so frightened? What didn't Allyson want Kristi to question Jaci about?

Kristi would be sure to mention the encounter to Jason. She felt sure Jaci hadn't told the sheriff everything she knew.

22

WEDNESDAY EVENING

For the second night in a row Jason's white Trail Blazer pulled into Kristi's driveway just after she did. She smiled as she unlocked the kitchen door. She could get used to having Jason around in the evenings. Especially if it meant he'd be around in the mornings too!

This time, the cats took his entrance in stride. Almost as if they'd discussed their strategy, Stitches wound around Kristi's legs while Between turned his purr-motor on full blast and rubbed against Jason's legs.

Jason glanced down at the little tuxedo cat in surprise before bending over and scooping the little fellow into his arms.

"You know, I've never seen the appeal of cats," he said, scratching behind Between's ears, "but I could get used to being greeted by a warm little fur-ball at the end of a long day."

Kristi leaned over to stroke Stitches before moving to the cabinet to get the cats' evening meal. "They're great company," she agreed. Then smiled and added, "But they're not the only ones who could greet you at the end of a long day…"

Jason placed Between back on the floor and moved to stand behind Kristi, putting his arms around her and drawing her back against his chest. "I definitely appreciate coming home to you," he murmured into her ear. "Even if that home is yours instead of ours."

She had to bite her lip to keep from saying, *We could change that, you know.*

Too soon. They'd only shared one night. They needed more time before either of them broached the idea of moving in together... or even the possibility of marriage. She reminded herself of her desire to take things slowly. To not rush into anything until they were sure.

But sleeping together had changed everything. She no longer wanted to tarry. Now that they'd claimed each other again in that most intimate way, she wanted to shout to the world that he was hers... and she was his!

She was fully committed to their relationship.

But was he?

Slow down, Kristi, she warned herself. Be sure of what he wants before you leap to the altar.

Stepping out of his embrace, she smiled at him as she put the cats' dinner down for them. Stitches and Between attacked their kibble as if she hadn't fed them for a week.

"Hungry little buggers, aren't they?" Jason said.

"Always. Speaking of hungry, what do you want for dinner?"

A wicked gleam lit his eyes, and he reached for her. "You!"

She laughed and pulled away. "I can be dessert," she teased. "What about dinner?"

"I'll call and order a pizza," he said, his voice low and rough, "if you'll make out with me on the couch while we wait for it to be delivered."

Desire shot through her core and she shivered. "That sounds," she paused and licked her lips, "wonderful."

He whipped his cell phone from its holster on his belt and made the call. Kristi raced to the front door, turned on the porch light, and made it back to the couch just as he ended the call.

"Now," he murmured, leaning over her as she perched on the couch cushion, "how does this go? I think I've forgotten."

"Here, let me show you." She grabbed his shirt, pulled him down next to her, and kissed him. After a moment she leaned back and grinned. "See? Nothing to it."

He grabbed her and pulled her into a tight embrace. "Maybe for you," he practically growled. "It's everything to me!"

He kissed her so passionately, she wanted nothing more than to shed her clothes and drag him into the bedroom. Damn the pizza!

Somehow, Kristi had no idea how, they managed to stay clothed until the doorbell rang. Jason growled his frustration while Kristi caught her breath.

"I'll get it," he said, studying her face. "You're lips look a bit puffy… and those bedroom eyes would give us away for sure."

Kristi rubbed a finger over her lips, but managed a knowing grin. "And yours won't?"

His brows drew together in what she thought of as his *cop face*. "I'm the sheriff," he said haughtily. "No one questions me."

She giggled as the doorbell rang again. "Sure. Whatever you say, *Sheriff*."

Jason strode to the door and yanked it open. "What?" he yelled.

"Uhm… your pizza?" the delivery kid sounded like he was barely old enough to drive.

Jason accepted the box, tipped the kid, and slammed the door in his face.

Kristi stood, stretched, and headed to the kitchen. "You could've been nicer," she called over her shoulder. "After all, the boy didn't do anything wrong."

"He interrupted us."

She laughed again. "We ordered the pizza," she pointed out. "That's pretty much *asking* to be interrupted."

"Yeah. Well. Where do you want this?"

"Just put it on the coffee table. I'm getting paper plates and napkins." She paused to pull those items out of the cabinet, then glanced at the refrigerator. "What do you want to drink? I have beer, cola, water, and iced tea."

"Beer," he said, appearing beside her. "I'll get the drinks."

She nodded. "Beer for me too."

When they were settled on the couch, sitting at opposite ends to keep from inadvertently touching, they loaded their plates with pizza and settled back to eat. Kristi grabbed the remote and turned on the TV, selecting a superhero movie.

"There," she said after a swallow of ice cold beer. "Dinner and a movie, just like civilized people."

He scowled at her. "I don't feel very civilized right now."

"I know," she said with a smile. "That's why we're pretending we care about who's winning the fight on screen."

He grunted.

The pizza was good, crisp crust, tangy sauce, spicy sausage, and lots of gooey cheese, but Kristi was eating by rote. All she really wanted was to finish her dinner and take Jason to bed. She was pretty sure... no she was *positive* that was all he was thinking about too.

She tried to eat slowly, chewing each bite thoroughly before swallowing. The last thing she wanted was to make herself sick. Throwing up while Jason was making love to her would be *so* unsexy!

When they finished their beer and pizza, Jason helped her put the leftovers away, then grabbed her hand and pulled her toward the bedroom.

She laughed and raced him to the bed. She'd toed off her shoes when his cell phone rang.

He paused, glanced at her with deep longing, then shook his head and answered the phone.

"Sheriff Reynolds." His expression darkened and he turned away from Kristi. "I'll be right there."

Picking up his gun belt, he buckled it back in place. Turning back to Kristi, he glanced at her, the bed, and then away. "I've got to go. There's been another poisoning."

Kristi gasped, her hands flying to her mouth. "No! Who? Are they all right?"

She followed him as he strode through the house to the kitchen, collected his Stetson and keys from the rack by the door, and paused. "It's Rhonda Gervais. She's been taken to the hospital. I don't know her condition yet." He touched the brim of his hat. "Don't wait up for me. I'll sleep in my own bed tonight... assuming I sleep at all."

And then he was gone.

Kristi slumped against the counter as Stitches and Between rubbed against her legs.

"Better get used to this, kitty-kids," she said quietly. "If we take Jason, we accept his job too." She picked up Stitches and rubbed her chin across the little tabby's head. "And with Jason, it's not just a job. It's who he is."

She needed to remember that before she jumped into anything more permanent.

She sighed. What did it matter? He was her man, the love of her life, and he was also a sheriff, through and through. He was a package deal... and she loved the whole package. They'd make it work.

23

THURSDAY MORNING

Early Thursday morning found Kristi driving her red Subaru Outback along Main Street. She was on her way to the fairgrounds to work the *Delectable Mountain Quilting* booth, but was in no hurry to arrive. She'd been slow to dress and leave the house that morning, taking extra time pulling on her favorite burgundy dress slacks with the stitched-in crease, a white silk blouse, and a lightweight navy cardigan all while carrying on a detailed, one-sided conversation with the cats.

The fact that Jason had been called away last night hadn't helped her mood. Nor had the fact that Rhonda Gervais had been poisoned!

It had been a long week and she was ready for the fair to end. Unfortunately, she wouldn't be able to close out her booth and return to simply running her shop until Sunday afternoon. She reminded herself that the booth had done a good business and that she'd found new customers, but somehow those facts didn't make up for the turmoil of the poisoned pickles. It might be years before she viewed the fair with anything other than trepidation.

Garnet Gateway wasn't feeling nearly as safe and secure as

she'd previously believed. Not with a seemingly insane poisoner on the loose.

So, when she stopped at a light and realized she was near *Roasted Beans*, she made a snap decision to stop for a glass of iced chai. Mattie was scheduled to work with her at the fair; if Kristi was a few minutes late, Mattie could handle it.

And Kristi would be better for a few minutes of relaxation with her favorite cold beverage.

Luck was with her and she found a parking space just down the block from the coffee shop. As she walked to the front door, she noticed Jaci Evans sitting at a table framed in the wide front window. Across from her was a teenage boy, but Kristi didn't recognize him. Jaci looked upset.

Well, of course she looked upset! Rhonda Gervais, the woman who had been poisoned last night, was her grandmother. Kristi barely knew Jaci, but she should still stop by her table and offer the girl her sympathy.

With that in mind, Kristi ordered her iced chai, then wound through the tables toward the front window. Before she could approach Jaci, the girl called her friend *Henry*.

Kristi paused. Could that be Henry Jenkins? Matt Jenkins' son? Matt... Herman Studebakker's partner and the second (well, fourth, actually) poisoning victim?

Suddenly, Kristi wanted to hear what the teens were saying more than she wanted to extend sympathy. She veered slightly to her right and took a seat at the table at the edge of the front window, which placed her right behind Jaci.

"I shouldn't have told you about Gramma telling me she'd seen me messing with the pickle jars," Jaci said, sniffling softly. "You told your dad, didn't you, Henry?" she accused, her voice hardening. "Don't bother denying it. He wouldn't have poisoned her if you hadn't."

Kristi's heart raced and her breath caught, but she forced herself to remain quiet. She'd heard enough to know that the kids at the next table were involved in the poisonings, but she wanted to learn more.

Her server arrived with her drink. "Here you go," the young woman said, placing the beverage on a coaster in front of Kristi. "One iced chai. Can I get you anything else?"

"No, thank you," Kristi responded quietly. When the young woman left, Kristi picked up her drink and sipped. The cool, creamy flavors of black tea, cinnamon, and ginger, with just the right amount of sweetness calmed her and she was able to refocus on the kids' conversation.

The boy, Henry, was speaking. "...didn't know. I never thought Dad would hurt your grandmother." He paused, and Kristi leaned back in her chair as if she could encourage him to continue by moving closer. "Of course, I didn't think he'd poison himself just to throw off the sheriff's investigation."

Kristi nodded to herself and took another sip of her chai. The boy was definitely Matt Jenkins' son. And Jason needed to know what Kristi had overheard.

She drank the rest of her iced chai as calmly as possible, then carried the empty cup to the trash. When her hands were free, she pulled her cell phone from its pocket in her embroidered denim shoulder bag and dialed Jason's number as she stepped out of *Roasted Beans* and onto the sidewalk. She was so engrossed in her phone, that she walked right into a man, who caught her arm to prevent her from stumbling.

"I'm so sorry," she said, looking up into the man's face. "Please forgive me!"

"Not a problem," he said. His voice was jovial, but his eyes held a dangerous glint. She tried to step away, but he held her arm firmly.

"You can let go now," she said. "I'm perfectly stable."

"You're many things, Ms. Lundrigan," the man said, his expression darkening, "but right now, stable isn't one of them."

Kristi's heart raced and her instincts shouted at her to run, but he held her firmly. She glanced around for someone to help her, but it was early enough that the sidewalk was empty. But she heard Jason pick up on her call. "Kristi?" he said, his voice sounding weak and tinny from where she held the phone at her side. "Are you there?"

Suddenly, she knew what to do. She needed to identify this man for Jason. She was fairly certain of his identity, but she needed to be sure.

"I'm sorry," she said again. "Do I know you?"

The man laughed, a thoroughly unpleasant sound. "No, but you're going to."

"You're Matt Jenkins, aren't you?"

The cell phone in her hand had gone silent. Kristi prayed that Jason was listening. He had to be listening!

"That's right," Matt said, "and I saw you listening to my idiot son and that stupid girl he likes." He shook a finger in her face. "Eavesdropping isn't a good look for you, Ms. Lundrigan." He yanked her arm, forcing her to follow him down the street. "Come along. We need to talk."

She tried again to pull away, but his grip was too tight; tried to plant her feet and resist his attempt to pull her to his car.

Matt stopped, turned toward her, and with the hand that wasn't clamped to her arm, brandished a pistol in her face. Yanking her even with him, he moved the gun until its nozzle pressed into her side.

Kristi gasped and her heart slammed against her chest. Her knees felt weak. She'd been shot once before. By Velma Carson, Mattie's deranged mother. She never wanted to repeat that experience.

"Come along quietly, Ms. Lundrigan. I don't want to have to shoot you, but I will." He glared at her, an ugly gleam in his eye. "And trust me, if you force me to that option, I'll make sure it's a fatal one."

She nodded, trying hard to regulate her breathing. The last

thing she wanted was to pass out from hyperventilation. She had to stay calm. Gripping her phone carefully so she wouldn't inadvertently end the call, she slipped it into the pocket of her trousers as inconspicuously as possible.

That phone was her lifeline, the only way Jason could know what was happening to her.

And she needed Jason to know!

24

THURSDAY MID-MORNING

The ride across town in Matt Jenkins' car was a nightmare.

He forced her to drive while he held the gun on her. Directed her to their destination with short, clipped comments. Hoping that Jason was still on the line and could hear her through the fabric of both her trouser pocket and the seat belt, she repeated each of Matt Jenkins' directions.

"What are you, deaf?" he asked after the her third repetition.

She chanced a quick side-eyed glance at him, but the sight of the gun unnerved her, so she kept her eyes on the road.

"No. I'm terrified. You're holding a gun on me!" She licked her lips before adding, "I talk when I'm nervous."

When he didn't respond, she steeled herself to continue repeating his directions… as loudly as she dared.

After what felt like an eternity they pulled behind a single story, cement block warehouse near the railroad tracks. Jenkins insisted she park as close to the building as she could.

"Out," he said, opening his own door without looking away from her. He waited until she stepped out of the car, then grabbed the keys from the ignition and jumped out as well. "Go stand by the door." He used the gun to motion toward the man door beside the padlocked loading dock.

Kristi complied. She didn't want to be here, but she didn't know what else to do. Not when he held a gun on her and she was in an area of Garnet Gateway she didn't know. She was blocks from the part of town where she knew all the streets and most of the businesses that lined them. She didn't even know if the warehouses that surrounded this one would be staffed during the day. What if they were empty except when their owners needed to load or unload something?

Too many unknowns to try to run. Besides, she knew for a fact she couldn't outrun a bullet. She'd tried that once before... and failed. She wasn't anxious to be shot again. Especially not since Matt had promised to make sure she didn't live through the experience.

Her only hope was the cell phone in her pocket. That the call was still active, and that Jason had been able to hear what was said.

A tenuous hope at best.

Matt held the gun on her with one hand while he unlocked the man door with the other. Pushing the door open, he gestured her inside. She glanced around, desperately seeking an avenue of escape. Finding nothing she hadn't already considered and rejected, she hugged herself and stepped into the warehouse. The interior was dark. The only windows were high on the front wall, barred, and very small. Cement block walls, cement floor underfoot, and the shadowy images of stacks of boxes and barrels.

The door closed behind her, making the shadows even deeper. Kristi whirled. Had he left her here alone? Her hand flew to her pocket, dreaming of Jason's voice. But before she could pull the cell phone out, light flooded the room.

Matt stood beside the door, one hand on the light switch, the other still pointing the gun in her direction. He stepped forward, grabbed her arm again and dragged her deeper into the maze of boxes. When she stumbled around one stack of barrels that smelled remarkably like pickles, she found herself in a cleared space with a single chair in the center.

"Sit," he ordered, waving the gun toward the chair.

Kristi sat.

"Now, tell me everything you heard the kids talking about."

Kristi's mind raced. What could she say? It hadn't sounded like the teens had intended to harm anyone, Henry even said he hadn't believed his dad would hurt Jaci's grandmother. Kristi didn't want to give this crazed man reason to harm those kids. But neither did she want him to shoot her! Maybe claiming ignorance would be the best for all involved.

"I-I don't know what you think I heard," Kristi said, struggling to keep her voice calm and even, "but I barely know Jaci Evans and I'd never seen that boy before. Was he your son? I assumed he was her boyfriend."

Matt's frown deepened and it sounded to Kristi like he snarled. God! She hoped Jason had heard everything and was on his way! Her heart and mind both raced. What if Jason wasn't coming? What if she had to rescue herself? She knew she'd never make it out of this warehouse alive, but she had to try. She refused to sit here and allow herself to be murdered.

Carefully, she leaned forward, curling in on herself as if in despair, but pulling her legs solidly beneath her center, ready to leap if the opportunity presented itself.

"Don't play dumb, Ms. Lundrigan. I could see through the window that the stupid girl was crying. She said something. Henry probably did too. He's too soft on her for his own good. You heard, or you wouldn't have hurried out so fast."

"I was late for the fair," Kristi whimpered, interrupting his rant. She rocked back and forth on her chair as if seeking comfort, but really testing her balance. "I have a booth at the fair, and I was hurrying because I was late."

He smirked. "Sure, sure. You were just in a hurry to get to the fair. Not to call your boyfriend, the sheriff." He waved the gun around, then slipped it into the waistband of his trousers. "Everyone knows you're sleeping with him. You probably couldn't wait to report what you heard." He paused and studied her, a disgusted expression crossing his face as he watched her performance. "Now, what was it? What did you hear?" He reached for the gun again. "Do you need a little incentive? Should I shoot off a finger to loosen your tongue?"

Fear spiked Kristi's heart rate and beads of sweat popped out on her forehead, but she settled into a crouched position. She'd have to launch herself at the man before he drew that gun.

Where was Jason?

"I wouldn't recommend that," a new voice said. A calm voice edged with danger. A voice Kristi would recognize anywhere. Jason was here!

Jenkins jerked around, searching for the speaker.

Kristi almost closed her eyes in relief. Almost. Instead she took advantage of Jenkins' distraction, hurled herself away from the chair, and bolted behind a stack of boxes.

"Hurting her in any way will put you in a world of danger." Jason stepped out from behind the pickle barrels, his Glock 22 held steady in a two-handed grip and pointed at Matt.

Matt's fingers tightened around the gun in his waistband, but Jason said, "Don't. I'd hate to have to shoot you, Jenkins. Put the gun on the ground and kick it away. Easy! Just use two fingers."

Matt snarled again, but did as he was told.

"Now, on your knees. Hands behind your head."

Kristi leaned against the stack of boxes, her body trembling in reaction. Once she was sure Jason was in control of the situation, she crept back around the corner and watched as Jason quickly and efficiently pulled Matt's hand's behind his back and hand-cuffed him.

Once the man was restrained, Jason's eyes sought Kristi. "Are you all right?"

She nodded and inhaled a shaky breath. "I am now. How did you find me?"

Deputy Millson stepped around the pickle barrels and took charge of Jenkins, freeing Jason to move to Kristi's side. He pulled her to standing and enveloped her in a tight hug.

After a moment, he released her and answered her question. "Two ways actually. You managed to leave your call open, good job, by the way, and…"

"And? And what?" she prompted when he didn't finish his sentence fast enough.

"And Henry Jenkins called."

Kristi's eyes widened in surprise. "Henry called?"

Jason nodded. "Said he'd seen his father force you into his car. He didn't want anyone else to get hurt."

Kristi nodded. "I thought he seemed like a good kid. How did his dad get him mixed up in this?"

Jason put his arm around her shoulders and guided her toward the door. "Let's get out of here," he said quietly. "I don't like thinking about what might've happened if I hadn't gotten here when I did."

She shivered and nodded in agreement.

"I'll tell you everything on the way to the station."

25

THURSDAY AFTERNOON

Kristi sat in the visitor chair across from Jason's desk at the sheriff's office. The pale green walls and old-fashioned teacher's desk were dingy and worn, but familiar and therefore comforting. This was Jason's office, and Jason meant safety. She was safe and healthy and so was Jason. All was right with her world.

She'd expected Jason to tell her everything that had led up to his rescue of her on the drive back to the station, but when she finally pulled her cell phone from her pocket and disconnected the call that had saved her life, she found numerous missed calls and voicemails from Mattie. The messages became more and more desperate sounding until the last one, when Mattie demanded to know where Kristi was and what had happened to her.

So instead of hearing all about how Jason had found her and what had happened while she'd been held captive by Matt, Kristi spent the drive to the sheriff's department calling Mattie, giving her the condensed version of the morning's events, and asking her to contact Andrea to come in and take Kristi's place at the fair. They'd also agreed that Mattie would change the schedule so that Kristi could spend Friday at the shop instead of at the fairgrounds.

By the time Kristi and Mattie had everything arranged, Jason was pulling the Trail Blazer into his parking slot at the sheriff's department. He'd walked Kristi to his office, given her a quick hug and a kiss, and then disappeared into the building to deal with Matt Jenkins and the rest of his duties.

Deputy Millson appeared at the office door. "Sheriff Reynolds says I should take you home."

Kristi shook her head. "No thanks. He promised he'd explain everything, but he hasn't had a chance. I'll wait."

Janet Millson grinned, her dark eyes dancing with mischief. "Yep. He figured you'd say that. I'm supposed to show you back to the observation room so you can watch the interrogation."

Kristi frowned. "I thought you said he wanted you to take me home."

Millson shrugged. "It was worth a try."

Kristi stared at the dark-haired young woman who was Jason's second in command. She was a very competent law enforcement officer, but she had a streak of mischief that kept Jason— and now Kristi, it seemed— on his toes. "I can't believe you said that! You're a scamp."

"I am," Millson said with a grin. "Well, come on if you're coming."

The deputy led Kristi to a small, dimly lit room with a few chairs and a large window looking onto a room with a metal table and two chairs, one on each side. The window, a one-way mirror, brightened as Jason stepped into the room carrying a manila file folder stuffed with papers and flipped the light switch. He was followed by Matt Jenkins, now wearing an orange jumpsuit, with his hands cuffed in front of him.

Jenkins sat on one side of the table, Jason on the other.

"For the record this is Sheriff Jason Reynolds interviewing Matthew Jenkins in the matter of the poisoning death of Herman

Studebakker, as well as the poisonings of Louisa Rizzoli, Silvi Kuhlman, and Rhonda Gervais. He is also charged with unlawful detention of Kristi Lundrigan and intimidation of Jaci Evans and Henry Jenkins."

Jason shuffled through his papers while Jenkins slouched on the other side of table, looking remarkably relaxed.

"Let's start with the unlawful detention case. That one is indisputable. You were apprehended with Ms. Lundrigan in your warehouse, and she has pressed charges. Why did you detain Ms. Lundrigan?"

Jenkins glanced at Sheriff Reynolds and shrugged. "He said, she said. She says I *detained* her, I say she came with me willingly."

The sheriff nodded. "And why did she accompany you to that warehouse?"

"For sex, of course." Jenkins smirked. "Everyone knows she's a whore. She just needed a little before work pick-me-up."

Kristi gasped and turned to Deputy Millson. "Why that lying scum!"

Janet Millson shushed her and pointed back to the window. "The sheriff will handle it."

Jason's jaw tightened. "I see. And how did you arrange for this... assignation?"

Jenkins straightened in his chair, clearly enjoying this line of questioning. "We just happened to meet on the street. She propositioned me." He shrugged again. "I'm a healthy man; I wasn't going to turn down a quick tumble."

"And you thought a warehouse was a... comfortable venue for your *tumble?*"

"Whatever," Jenkins said with another smirk. "Once she was on her back, I'd have all the padding I needed."

Kristi fumed, her blood boiling. She wanted nothing more than to storm into that room and slap the smirk off that, that *beast's* face!

"Let's move on to the poisonings," Jason said, his jaw tight with anger, but his voice calm and reasonable. "We have eye witness testimony that you coerced a fair volunteer, Jaci Evans, into exchanging a legitimate entry of dill pickles with a jar you provided."

"Your witness is mistaken. I've never spoken to the girl."

"But you know who she is?"

"I'd have to check with Henry, but I believe she's one of his friends."

"Henry? Are you referring to your son, Henry Jenkins?"

"Yes."

Jason nodded. "Would it surprise you to learn that Henry, your son, called our dispatcher this morning when he saw you force Ms. Lundrigan into your car?"

Jenkins surged to his feet. "That's a lie! Henry would never inform on me!"

Jason leaned back in his chair, looking completely at ease. "Henry also told us about the jar of pickles, and about how you sprinkled a bit of dried hemlock on your spaghetti at Rizzoli's. Not enough to kill yourself, just enough to make you sick and avert suspicion."

Jenkins paced the length of the table, then kicked the chair sideways and sat down again. "No. He didn't."

"He did," Jason said firmly. "He also told us how you poisoned Rhonda Gervais after he told you that she had confronted her granddaughter, Jaci Evans, about Jaci's likely involvement in the poisoning of the judges." Jason paused for a beat. "That was a mistake, you know. Jaci and Henry were too frightened to come to me... until you poisoned her grandmother. That action stiffened the girl's spine."

An expression of disgust crossed Jenkins' face. "Pshaw. That girl has no spine." He closed his eyes for a moment, his brows knit in a frown. "Lawyer," he said. "I want a lawyer."

Jason closed his file and rose. "This interview is terminated. The suspect has invoked his right to an attorney." He stepped to the door, opened it and beckoned. A deputy joined him at the door. "Lawson, please take Mr. Jenkins back to the detention center. Make sure he has access to a phone to contact an attorney."

Deputy Lawson nodded. "Yes, sir." Crossing to Jenkins, he led the man from the room.

In the observation room, Kristi turned to Deputy Millson. "You know, I can't quite see Matt Jenkins canning pickles, with or without adding hemlock. If you haven't already, you might want to question Vivi Rawlins."

Millson cocked her head. "Who's that?"

"She works at the Brewpub. If she grew up on a ranch, she might well know how to make pickles, and have the equipment to do it."

Millson considered a moment, then nodded. "That's a good thought, Kristi. I'll look into it."

Just then the observation room door opened and Jason stepped in. As he crossed to Kristi, Deputy Millson stepped out and closed the door behind her.

Jason folded his arms around Kristi and kissed her forehead. "I'm sorry you had to hear his allegations. They won't hold up and if I have anything to say about it, they won't come out in court."

She snuggled closer to him. "Don't worry about it. He made me mad, but fortunately I wasn't close enough to hit him."

"I was." He sighed. "But there are rules about beating a suspect unconscious during an interrogation." He held her at arms' length and smiled grimly. "But believe me, I wanted to."

"Good," she said with a feral grin. "I'm content with the thought." She paused for a moment, then asked, "What's next? Are you finished for the day?"

"Unfortunately, no. I need to meet with the county prosecutor and discuss what else she needs. Ms. Vanderhaven is a stickler, but she rarely loses at trial."

Kristi nodded. "We sure don't want Jenkins to get away with all of this."

"Definitely not. Listen, why don't I have one of my deputies drive you home? I'll come by as soon as I can. Okay?"

"Okay. But I need to retrieve my car, so I don't really need a ride. I'll just walk down to *Roasted Beans*."

Jason looked like he was going to object, but Kristi placed a finger over his lips. "It's just a couple of blocks, and I can't think of anyone else who'd want to kidnap me."

He growled, but nodded. "Just do me a favor? Text me once you're in the car, and again when you're safely in the house with your guard cats."

She laughed. "Will do. Now go figure out how to tie Jenkins up in a nice tight bow for the prosecutor!"

After a more thorough kiss, he opened the observation room door and walked with her to the front entrance.

"Don't forget," he said sternly. "Two texts!"

"I'll remember," she said and stepped out onto Main Street's sidewalk.

26

THURSDAY NIGHT

It was nearly 10:00 P.M. before Jason made it home to Kristi. She was already in her favorite pale blue cotton pajamas, but had not yet gone to bed. Instead she was snuggled into the corner of her couch watching a movie she'd seen so often she nearly had the dialogue memorized.

Stitches curled against her leg, while Between stretched across her lap. Jason had been right to call them her guard cats. From the moment she'd walked in the kitchen door, the pair of them had been glued to her side. She wondered what clues she'd given off that had engaged their protective senses? Had they felt her anxiety? Smelled the remnants of fear? Or were they just telepathic? Whatever. They'd known she needed comfort and had done their best to provide it.

When Jason knocked, both cats leapt to the back of the couch and watched warily as she opened the door. As soon as they heard his voice, they relaxed and moved away, as if to say, *We're off duty. Your turn.*

Kristi had barely closed the door behind him before Jason pulled her into his arms and simply held her tightly. "I was so worried earlier," he murmured into her hair. "I wasn't sure I'd find you in time."

She buried her face in his chest and nodded, breathing in the familiar scent of him, musk and sage and… strength. "I knew you'd find me," she whispered, "but I was still terrified. He was just so… unhinged."

After a moment, they broke apart and she led him to the couch. "Sit," she said, grabbing the remote and turning off the TV. "I'll get you a beer. Do you need food? I can make you a sandwich."

He tossed his Stetson on the coffee table and collapsed onto the couch, rubbing his eyes. "Beer, yes. Food, no. I caught a bite with the prosecutor."

When they were both settled with a cold beer, Kristi asked, "So what happened? Does Ms. Vanderhaven think you have a case?"

Jason sipped his beer before answering. "Definitely. That suggestion you gave Millson was gold. She pulled Vivi Rawlins in for questioning and the woman cracked before Millson even had a chance to ask the hard questions."

Kristi stared at him, eyes wide and mouth open. After a moment she shook herself and said, "Really? She was involved? I was totally guessing."

His eyes gleamed with amusement, or maybe it was pride, but he said, "Well, guess, intuition, whatever, it was right on target." He took another swig of his beer. "She grew up on one of the outlying ranches. Her dad was a ranch hand, but her mom did the cooking for the men who worked the cattle. She and the rancher's wife canned every autumn and Vivi helped from the time she was old enough to pick vegetables from the garden." He paused, rolled the beer bottle across his forehead, seeming to enjoy the coolness of the condensation, then continued. "And get this… pickles were her mom's specialty."

"But, why?" Kristi asked. "Why would she add hemlock to those pickles? Anyone on a ranch would recognize that weed. They have to protect the cattle from its poison. She had to have known it wasn't dill." She paused and sipped her beer thoughtfully. "I mean, some city woman unfamiliar with the land might mistake hemlock for dill, they do look similar, but no ranch woman would."

He shook his head. "It was no mistake. She knew what she was doing. Evidently she and Jenkins were involved. He was angry with Herman Studebakker and talked her into poisoning the pickles by telling her it was a prank— remember that, you'll hear it again. She expected Herman to react the same way the two women did, get violently ill, but recover quickly. Jenkins knew different."

"Are you sure? Maybe he was just trying to scare Herman. I mean, everyone knows Herman was a little over the top about pickles."

"Oh, Jenkins knew. He confessed as much to Rawlins after Studebakker died. She was horrified, and more than a little frightened of the man she'd been sleeping with. That fear is part of the reason she confessed so readily. She wants to see him put away as badly as we do."

"But I thought Studebakker and Jenkins were partners? What did Herman do to make Matt decide to kill him? And how did he know the hemlock would kill Herman, but not either of the women?"

Jason leaned his head back and closed his eyes. "Greed, pure and simple. Herman was ready to retire. He was looking for someone to buy out his share of the business. Jenkins couldn't come up with the cash to buy him out, but their partnership papers had a *successors clause* stating that if one partner died, the other would inherit his interests in the company." He paused for a moment. "As to how he knew the poison would be fatal... Jenkins knew about Herman's heart medication. The techs found research on his computer about drug interactions and what not to mix with what."

"That's... horrible."

Kristi set her beer bottle on a coaster on the coffee table and clasped her hands together. She'd begun to shiver as she listened, but didn't want to distract Jason from his tale.

"What about Henry and Jaci?" she asked quietly. "How did they get involved?"

"Jenkins used the *just a prank* line on them too. He'd been trying to figure out how to switch the jars of pickles when he overheard Henry talking to his girlfriend about being a volunteer for the judging. He talked Henry into getting Jaci to switch the jars. Which also meant Jenkins didn't even need to be at the fair to carry out his scheme. If anyone's fingerprints were going to be on that jar, they wouldn't be his."

Kristi's shivering increased until her teeth were chattering. She'd been taken captive by that man. She could've died!

Jason must have heard the chattering, because he opened his eyes, sat up, and studied her. "What's wrong, sweetheart?" He scooted across the couch until he was close beside her, put an arm around her and exclaimed, "You're shivering! Are you sick?"

She shook her head, trying to calm her racing heart. "N-no, just..." Just what, she wondered. Jason had rescued her hours ago. Why was she reacting now?

He pulled her into his lap and rubbed her arms. "You're okay," he murmured. "You're safe. It's just a reaction to everything that happened today. I should've been paying more attention when I told you all that. It's okay. It's over. He's behind bars and Ms. Vanderhaven assures me he's not going to escape prison. He can't hurt you now."

He kissed the top of her head and held her until the shivers receded and she relaxed against his chest.

"I'm sorry," she whispered. "That was... unexpected."

"Nothing to be sorry about. You held up beautifully all day."

He paused a moment. "Maybe too beautifully. Since you hadn't reacted earlier, I wasn't prepared for it now."

"I'm okay now," she said, but made no effort to disentangle herself from his arms. "What will happen to Henry and Jaci? Are they in trouble?"

"Well, they should've come forward sooner, but Jaci was terrified she'd be arrested for murder, and Henry was set on protecting her. But then his dad went too far. When he poisoned her grandmother, they decided they had to tell the truth, no matter what. And then Henry happened to look out the window and see, well, your predicament and they called 9-1-1."

He kissed her forehead. "Ms. Vanderhaven decided they'd been instrumental in your rescue, had suffered enough at Jenkins' hands, and were really only guilty of being gullible kids. She decided not to charge them, but gave them a stern talking to and warned them to stay out of trouble in the future."

Kristi nodded. "That's good." She was tired, so very tired, but she was so comfortable in Jason's arms she didn't want to move. She just wanted to close her eyes and sleep. Pretend all of this had just been a bad dream.

She wasn't sure when he did it, but Jason picked her up, carried her to bed, then tucked her in. She woke once in the wee hours of the morning to find him sleeping peacefully beside her, one arm thrown possessively across her middle. She smiled, snuggled closer to him, and drifted back to sleep.

27

FRIDAY - EPILOGUE

After all the excitement and terror of the day before, Kristi almost felt like she was sleep-walking through the day on Friday. She put in her hours with Ruby at the shop, while Mattie and Andrea handled the booth at the fair. Kristi knew she was blessed in her employees, both full-time and temporary. They took care of everything, including her, that day. She was too distracted to be of much use, but Ruby took up the slack and handled the customers with ease.

Kristi was more than ready for the fair to be done, but there were still two and a half days before they could pack up the booth on Sunday afternoon and put the whole experience in the past. Fortunately, it would be a few months before she had to make a decision about whether or not to participate next year. Right now, she wasn't sure she'd ever feel good about setting foot on the fairgrounds again.

But that was a stupid feeling. She still had to work the booth on Sunday morning and pack out in the afternoon.

Still, once she left…

She shook her head to clear the fog of thoughts that crowded her mind. Murder. Pickles. Poison. Deadly pranks. None of it mattered now. The crime had been solved. The perpetrators were in cells awaiting trial. And the victims were recovering.

All but poor Herman. Whose only crimes had been a love of pickles and a desire to retire.

But she, Kristi, was alive and well and even if she was walking around in a fog today, she had a date with Jason tonight. Dinner at *Rizzoli's Fine Italian Restaurant*, where she hoped Mama Rizzoli would soon be well enough to greet her guests again.

Jason appeared just as Ruby was flipping the *Open* sign to *Closed*.

Ruby grinned and waved him inside before locking the front door. "You just made it," she teased.

"I could've always pounded on the door and shouted 'Open up in the name of the law!'" He threw Ruby a grin and strode to the back to where Kristi was pulling her embroidered denim shoulder bag out of a locker.

"Ready for dinner?" he asked.

She smiled. "Definitely."

"Then let's go."

Since it was a lovely summer evening, they walked the four blocks from the shop on Park Street to *Rizzoli's* on Main. As she walked, the fog lifted from Kristi's mind and she smelled cut grass sweetened with the scents of the flowers lining the walks of the shops they passed. She savored the blue of a sky not yet bleeding into sunset, the majestic mountains rising in the distance, and the quiet rumble of distant traffic.

And Jason's strong, secure presence holding her hand.

Jason. Her love. Her life.

When they reached *Rizzoli's*, Kristi was surprised and delighted to see Mama seated in a throne-like chair overseeing her domain. They were shown to a table near the front window, but before being seated they went to greet the owner.

"You look wonderful, Mrs. Rizzoli," Jason said, leaning in to kiss her weathered cheek. "I hope you're feeling well."

She took his hand and gripped it tightly. "I am, thanks to you."

"Me?" Jason's brow lifted in surprise. "You mean your doctors, surely."

"No. I mean you," Mama said. "You caught the terrible man who caused us so much pain. You made me feel safe again. In my home. In my business. In my town." She nodded and glanced around the room, meeting the eyes of each of her servers and staff. They all stopped what they were doing and moved closer to Mama.

"We, the Rizzoli family and restaurant staff owe you a debt of gratitude. Thank you, Sheriff Reynolds."

A flush rose up Jason's neck and spread to his cheeks. Kristi took his hand and squeezed. She knew he wasn't accustomed to public acclamation. If anything, he was more used to criticism than praise. An individual might thank him privately now and then, but nothing like this. Nothing this public. Every eye in the restaurant was turned on him. Staff, patrons, everyone.

And then, they all began to clap.

It started with Mama's husband, Salvatore Rizzoli, but the sound just kept growing as person after person stood and applauded Jason.

He released Kristi's hand and turned in a slow circle, gazing at the folk of Garnet Gateway. His town. His county. His people. Citizens he was sworn to protect.

He swallowed convulsively, held up his hands, and waited. When the room stilled, he spoke.

"Thank you, Mrs. Rizzoli, everyone. I appreciate your thanks, but this isn't necessary. I'm just doing the job you all elected me to do." He turned to Mama. "I'm glad you're feeling safe again, Mrs. Rizzoli," he said quietly, "but let's just get on with eating your fine food."

She held out her hand to him, and he put his large, calloused one in her small wrinkled one. She gripped it tightly, then patted it with her other hand.

"Yes," she said with a smile. "Go and order your dinner. Whatever you want. Your money is no good here, tonight."

"No, ma'am," he said, his face and voice serious. "Law enforcement officers in this county pay their own way, and that includes me. I thank you for the thought, though."

"Such an upright man," she said, releasing his hand. "You make me proud to live here, Sheriff." She leaned a little to the side and met Kristi's gaze. "You have a fine man, here, Kristi Lundrigan." She smiled. "You are a blessing to him, and he is lucky to have you in his life." She waved them away. "Now go. Enjoy your meal."

When they were seated, Jason reached across the table for Kristi's hand. "She's right, you know," he said quietly. "You are a blessing to me."

The server stopped at their table and Jason glanced up. "Give us a few minutes, please." The young woman nodded and turned away. Jason said, "Thank you."

He turned back to Kristi. "I've been thinking about it," he said, studying her with an intense gaze. "I like coming home to you after a hectic day. I especially like waking up beside you in the morning. Hell, I even like your cats." He paused, swallowed, and squeezed her hand. "Will you marry me, Kristi. Again. I've…."

She shushed him and held out her other hand to him. "Of course I will. I've been hoping this was where we were heading."

His eyes widened and he licked his lips. "Really?"

She nodded. "Really."

A wide smile lit his face, only to disappear as fast as it had bloomed.

"What?" she asked, concern etching her expression.

"Well," he said, glancing at the table. "It's just that I didn't plan this right. I don't have a ring for you."

She giggled and he glanced up at her.

"That's okay," she said. "I don't need a ring."

"Oh, yes you do," he said, a fierce light in his eyes. "And not the one I gave you before. We're getting all new rings this time around."

She nodded. "Yes."

He squeezed her hands before nodding to the server. "We'll visit Kaufmann's Jewelry first thing tomorrow. For now, let's order dinner." He turned to the server as she approached the table. "We're celebrating. Bring us a bottle of your best champagne!"

The young woman smiled. "Right away, sir."

Kristi glanced over Jason's shoulder to where Mama Rizzoli sat on her throne-like chair observing them carefully. The older woman nodded and mouthed a single word: *Congratulations!*

Kristi grinned and turned her attention back to Jason.

Her world. Her love. Her affianced husband!

What a great end to a stressful week. Poisoned pickles were just a crime to be solved, but Jason... Jason was her life.

ALSO BY DEBBIE MUMFORD

Kristi Lundrigan Mysteries:

- DELECTABLE MOUNTAIN QUILTING (NOVEL)
- IN A PICKLE (NOVEL)
- DOUBLE WEDDING RING (NOVEL - PREORDER NOW!)
- FOOL'S PUZZLE (SHORT STORY)
- WILDFIRE! (SHORT STORY)
- CHRISTMAS STAR (SHORT STORY)

Gus and Ghost Short Story Series:

- SEVENTH
- SEVENTH: FIRST FRUITS
- DEATH OF AN ALCHEMIST (UNCOLLECTED ANTHOLOGY)
- SEVENTH: THE SAMHAIN DILEMMA
- DARK OF THE MOON (UNCOLLECTED ANTHOLOGY)
- FLIGHT PLAN (UNCOLLECTED ANTHOLOGY)

Logans of Lastalrig Series:

- HER HIGHLAND LAIRD (NOVELLA)
- HER HIGHLAND YULE (SHORT STORY)

Red's Series:

- RED'S MAGICK (SHORT STORY COLLECTION)
- SEEING RED (SHORT STORY)

Signs of the Prophecy Novels:

- YOUNGEST

- SEEKER
- CHOSEN (COMING SOON!)

Sorcha's Children Series:

- SORCHA'S CHILDREN (OMNIBUS EDITION)
- SORCHA'S HEART (NOVELLA)
- DRAGONS' CHOICE (NOVEL)
- DRAGONS' FLIGHT (NOVEL)
- DRAGONS' DESIRE (NOVEL)
- DRAGONS' DESTINY (NOVEL)

Supernatural Yellowstone Short Story Series:

- REALITY BITES
- THE CAT LADY OF YELLOWSTONE

Uncollected Anthology Short Stories:

- DEATH OF AN ALCHEMIST (UA ALCHEMY)
- THE WEDDING CAKE (UA MAGICAL ARTS)
- DARK OF THE MOON (UA PARANORMAL PIRATES)
- IN THE BANYAN COPSE (UA UNEXPECTED HISTORIES)
- OLD ONE (UA MAGICAL QUESTS)
- HAVE HOARD, WILL SEEK (UA A DIVERSITY OF DRAGONS)
- FLIGHT PLAN (UA MYSTICAL MAPS)
- DISAPPEARED! (UA WERE-CREATURES & CONUNDRUMS)

Universal Star League Short Story Series:

- VOYAGES INTO THE BLACK (COLLECTION)
- THE WARBIRDS OF ABSAROKA
- AWAKENING THE WARRIOR
- INCIDENT ON THE ODYSSEY
- THE QUEEN'S CAPTIVE
- THE LOST COLONY

- Freighter Families in Space

Witchling Short Story Series:

- Witchling
- The Solitary Sorceress
- To Protect a Princess

Stand Alone Novels:

- Second Sight

Historical Fiction:

- Her Highland Laird (Novella)
- Her Highland Yule
- Incident on the High Line
- Miss Bainbridge's Summer Adventure
- Miss Bainbridge's Christmas Party
- Sisters in Suffrage
- The Trail Where We Cried
- The White Dragon and the Red

Short Story Collections:

- Love in a Flash
- Tales of Bygone Days
- Tales of Love & Magick
- Tales of the Unexpected
- Tales of Tomorrow
- Tales of Disastrous Deeds

Short Fiction:

- A Grove of Mountain Ash
- A Walk with Georgia

- AN ALIEN ADVENTURE
- ASTROMANCER
- BECAUSE OF THE CHRISTMAS STROLL
- BENEATH AND BEYOND
- DEEP DREAMING
- DELIA'S DECISION
- EGG THIEF
- ENCHANTMENT, INC.
- ICE STORM
- INCIDENT ON THE HIGH LINE
- IN SEARCH OF A VALENTINIAN
- IZZIE
- JOLLY WELL DONE
- KEYSTROKES & INTUITION
- MISS BAINBRIDGE'S CHRISTMAS PARTY
- MISS BAINBRIDGE'S SUMMER ADVENTURE
- NEEDLE-GREEN
- NEW YEAR
- OPENING HER EYES
- REMEMBRANCE
- SILVER-TIPPED DEATH
- SIMON SAYS
- SISTERS IN SUFFRAGE
- SKYE DREAMS
- SPINNING
- THE TIE THAT BINDS
- THE TRAIL WHERE WE CRIED
- THE WHITE DRAGON AND THE RED
- TO DREAM OF FLYING
- TREASURES
- TRIAL ON THE TRAIL
- WAKINYAN'S VALLEY

"WDM Presents" Anthologies:

- SPUN YARNS UNWOUND, VOL. 1
- SPUN YARNS UNWOUND: VOL. 2
- SPUN YARNS UNWOUND: VOL. 3

WATCH FOR DOUBLE WEDDING RING

If you enjoyed *In a Pickle*, be sure to watch for *Double Wedding Ring*, the third installment of the Kristi Lundrigan Mystery trilogy.

Here's what it's all about:

Kristi's life is busy and a little hectic as she plans her Thanksgiving holiday. It's not just the Double Wedding Ring quilt she and her staff are working on… it's also the fact that murder keeps rearing its ugly head. This time on the town's prize carousel!

What's a quilter to do?

Double Wedding Ring is scheduled for release in late October, 2024. Watch for it at your favorite online retailer.

ABOUT DEBBIE MUMFORD

Debbie Mumford specializes in speculative fiction (fantasy, paranormal romance, and science fiction) as well as mystery and historical fiction. Author of the popular *Sorcha's Children* series, Debbie loves the unknown, whether it's the lure of space or earthbound mythology. Her work has been published in multiple volumes of *Fiction River*, as well as in *Heart's Kiss Magazine*, *Amazing Monster Tales*, and many other popular anthologies. She writes about dragon-shifters, time-traveling lovers, and detectives—whether amateur or professional—for adults as Debbie Mumford, and science fiction and fantasy for tweens and young adults as Deb Logan.

Join Debbie's special announcement newsletter list and receive a FREE story!

To learn more, visit Debbie at:
debbiemumford.com/
Or send her an email at:
deborah.mumford@gmail.com

f facebook.com/DebbieMumfordWrites
a amazon.com/author/debbiemumford
BB bookbub.com/authors/debbie-mumford
X x.com/deborah_mumford

www.ingramcontent.com/pod-product-compliance
Lightning Source LLC
Chambersburg PA
CBHW030342180626
46812CB00007B/2721